THE SPIES

Also by Luis Fernando Verissimo in English translation:

The Club of Angels

Borges and the Eternal Orangutans

Luis Fernando Verissimo

THE SPIES

Translated from the Portuguese by
Margaret Jull Costa

MACLEHOSE PRESS
QUERCUS · LONDON

First published in the Portuguese language as *Os Espiões*
by Editora Objectiva Ltda in 2009
First published in Great Britain in 2012 by MacLehose Press
This paperback edition published in 2013 by

MacLehose Press
an imprint of Quercus
55 Baker Street
7th Floor, South Block
London W1U 8EW

Published by arrangement with Agência Riff and
Literarische Agentur Mertin Inh. Nicole Witt e.K., Frankfurt am Main, Germany
Copyright © 2009 by Luis Fernando Verissimo

English translation copyright © 2012 by Margaret Jull Costa
Illustrations copyright © Nelly Dimitranova

Obra publicada com apoio do Ministério da Cultura do Brasil / Fundação Biblioteca Nacional
Work published with support from the Brazilian Ministry of Culture / National Library Foundation

MINISTÉRIO DA CULTURA
Fundação BIBLIOTECA NACIONAL

The moral right of Luis Fernando Verissimo to be
identified as the author of this work has been
asserted in accordance with the Copyright,
Designs and Patents Act, 1988.

Margaret Jull Costa asserts her moral right to be identified as
the translator of the work.

A CIP catalogue record for this book is available
from the British Library

ISBN (MMP) 978 0 85705 114 1
ISBN (Ebook) 978 0 85738 437 9

10 9 8 7 6 5 4 3 2 1

Designed and typeset in Collis by Libanus Press, Marlborough
Printed and bound in Great Britain by Clays Ltd, St Ives plc

What shall I love unless it be the enigma?

GIORGIO DE CHIRICO

1

I'M A LITERATURE GRADUATE AND SEEK OBLIVION IN DRINK. But I only drink at weekends. From Monday to Friday, I work for a publishing company, where one of my tasks is to examine the unsolicited manuscripts that arrive by every post; they come in through the windows, drop from the ceiling, push up through the floorboards or are dumped on my desk by Marcito, the owner of the publishing house, with the words: "See if this one's any good." This festering deluge of authors seeking a publisher began after a little book of ours, entitled *Astrology and Love – A Sidereal Guide for Lovers*, proved such a success that Marcito was able to buy two new motorbikes for his collection. All those would-be writers suddenly became aware of our existence, and the torrent of manuscripts has never let up. It falls to me to decide their future. On Mondays, I always have a hangover, and any typescripts that arrive go straight from my trembling hands into the bin. And on Mondays, my rejection letters are particularly ferocious. I not only advise the author never to send us anything else, I also suggest that he or she never writes another line, another word – not even a receipt. If *War and Peace* were to arrive on my desk on a Monday, I would tell its author to take up gardening. Cervantes? Give it up, man. Flaubert? Proust? Don't make me laugh. Graham Greene? Consider a career in pharmacy. Not even le Carré would escape. I once advised a woman called Corina to concentrate on her housework and spare the world her demented belief that she was a poet. One day, she barged into my office, brandishing the rejected book, which had ended up being published by someone else, and hurled it at my head. Whenever anyone asks me where I got the small scar over my left eye, I say: "Poetry."

Corina has since published several books of poetry and *pensées* with great success. She makes a point of sending me invitations to her various launches and signings. I understand her latest publication is a collection of her complete poetry and prose, four hundred pages of the stuff. In hardback. I live in fear that one day she'll turn up at the office and hurl that great brick at my head too.

A more immediate threat, at the time, came from Fulvio Edmar, the author of *Astrology and Love*, who had never received any royalties for his work. He had paid for the first edition himself and felt that he should receive full royalties for all the editions printed after the book took off. Marcito did not agree, and I was the one who had to respond to Fulvio Edmar's ever more outraged demands. For years, we exchanged insults by letter, although we never met. He once described to me in great detail how, if ever we did meet, he would put my testicles where my tonsils are. I, in turn, warned him always to carry a knuckleduster in his pocket.

However, even my most violent rejection letters, my Monday-morning diatribes, end with a charming postscript. On Marcito's instructions. *If, however, you would care to pay for the publication of your own book, the publisher will be delighted to review this evaluation etc., etc.* Marcito and I were at school together. Two spotty fifteen-year-olds. Knowing that I was the best in the class at writing essays, he invited me to pen some dirty stories which he then stapled together to make a book entitled *The Wanker*, to be rented out to anyone who wanted to take it home with them, on condition that they return it the following day – unstained. After we left school, we didn't see each other for years, until, that is, I sought him out on hearing that he had started his own publishing house. I had written a novel, for which I needed a publisher. And, no, it wasn't a dirty book. We had a good laugh about *The Wanker*, but Marcito said that unless I paid for the publication costs myself there was no way he would publish a spy story about a fictitious Brazilian nuclear programme sabotaged by the Americans. The publishing house was only just getting started. His partner in the company was an uncle of his, who owned a fertiliser factory, and whose sole interest in the enterprise was the publication of a monthly almanac to be distributed among his customers in provincial Rio Grande do Sul. But then Marcito made me an offer. He had plans to start a real publishing house and needed someone to help him. If I went to work for him, he would eventually publish my novel. He couldn't promise me a large salary, but . . . At that point, I recalled that he had never once shared the money from *The Wanker* with me. He was doubtless going to exploit me again. But I was seduced by the idea of working for a publisher. I was, after all, a literature graduate, and, at the time, working in a shop selling videos. I was thirty years old and had recently married Julinha. João (Julinha wouldn't allow me to call him le Carré) was about to be born. So I agreed. That was twelve years ago. My first task was to copy out an encyclopaedia article about chameleons for inclusion in the almanac. A prophetic choice: the chameleon is a creature that adapts to any situation and merges into the background. That is precisely what I've been doing ever since. I read manuscripts. I write letters. I come up with most of the copy for an almanac intended to boost the sales of fertilisers. I feel sorry for myself and I drink. And, very slowly, I'm merging into the background.

The publishing house prospered. I discovered that there was more to Marcito than the cretinous rich kid I had always imagined him to be. He had a passion – which I would never have suspected in a collector of motorbikes – for Simenon. Since the success of *Astrology and Love*, we've published more books, mostly paid for by the authors themselves. If we're lucky or if the author has a large family, some of these books even sell quite well. Occasionally, I recommend that we publish one of the unsolicited manuscripts, especially if it arrives on a Friday, when I am full of good will towards humanity and its literary pretensions because I know that I will end the day at a table in the Bar do Espanhol, where my weekly booze-up begins, my three days of consciousness numbed by the *cachaça* and beer with which I cut myself free from myself and *mi puta vida* – my wretched life. My most frequent companion at that table in the Bar do Espanhol is Joel Dubin, who comes into the office twice a week, on Wednesdays and Fridays, to edit the almanac or check the proofs of any forthcoming books. They say that despite his short stature, his blue eyes thrill the girls at the college where he teaches Portuguese. He swears blind that he has never had it off with any of his students, although he does promise wild nights of love to those who manage to pass the university entrance exam. I know little about Dubin's actual sex life, except that it must be better than mine. Even the chairs in the Bar do Espanhol have a better sex life than I do. Dubin always used to fall in love with entirely unsuitable girls. Once, he was in the middle of an argument with one such girl when she asked the waiter if they had any sparkling wine without the bubbles. Dubin decided there and then that she wasn't safe out in the world on her own, and they very nearly got married. He wrote poems, bad poems. He introduced himself as "Joel Dubin, minor poet". He used to recite one of these poems to any potential girlfriend, something about a hypotenuse in search of a triangle. He called this his "geometrical chat-up line". Girls who understood the poem or smiled just to please him would immediately be rejected, because he loathed intellectuals. He preferred girls who bawled: "What?!"

Dubin and I had long arguments, at the office and at our table in the bar, about literature and grammar. We disagreed radically about the placement of commas. Dubin is a legalist and says that there are rules regarding the use of commas and that these should be respected. I am a relativist: I think that commas are like hundreds and thousands, to be distributed judiciously wherever they are needed and without spoiling one's enjoyment of the cake. It's not uncommon for me to re-revise Dubin's revision of a text and either cut out any commas he has added or add a few of my own in defiance of the rules, wherever I think fit. In the bar, our conversations used to begin with the comma and then branch out to take in the human condition and the universe. These debates would become increasingly vitriolic and strident the more we drank, until the Spaniard who owned the bar – hence the name – would come over and ask us to please keep the noise down. We would heap ever more rancorous insults on every writer in the city. I still don't know if Dubin accompanied me to the very depths of my weekly plunges into oblivion. I don't even know how I got home on Friday nights. Perhaps Dubin, having drunk rather less, actually carried me. I've never asked. On Saturday evenings, we would find ourselves back at the same table in the Bar do Espanhol, where we would start getting drunk all over again and resume the same insane conversation. It was a way of dramatising our own inescapable mediocrity, a kind of mutual flagellation through banality. Dubin called these endless argu-ments "Pavannes for the living dead". On one occasion, we spent almost an hour yelling at each other over some grammatical query or other –

"Enclisis!"

"Proclisis!"

"Enclisis!"

"Proclisis!"

"Enclisis!"

"Proclisis!"

– until the Spaniard signalled to us from behind the bar to keep the noise down.

I also don't know how I managed to get home in the early hours of Sunday morning. I spent all of Sunday sleeping, while Julinha and João went to lunch at her sister's house.

I was left alone with Black the dog. The sweet Julinha whom I married when she became pregnant had disappeared, never to be seen again, inside a fat, embittered woman of the same name. On Sundays, she only left food for the dog. If I wanted to eat, I had to negotiate with Black. Julinha hardly spoke to me at all. João, who was twelve, didn't talk to me either. The only one who did was Black. Well, his eyes seemed to say "I understand, I understand". On Sunday evenings, I would return to the Bar do Espanhol to meet up with Dubin. The Spaniard, by the way, isn't Spanish. His name is Miguel, but Professor Fortuna started calling him Don Miguel and then "the Spaniard". Equally, Professor Fortuna is not a professor. He was a regular at the bar, but never sat at our table.

He said that he didn't like to mix, not with us personally, but with humanity in general. He explained that he called the Spaniard "the Spaniard" because he reminded him of Miguel de Unamuno, whom he had, in fact, met. Now, as far as we knew, Unamuno had never visited Porto Alegre and the Professor had never left Porto Alegre. Sometimes we wondered if he had ever even left the Bar do Espanhol. Besides, the chronology didn't make sense, even though the Professor is a lot older than me or Dubin. "A bluffer" was what he called Unamuno. We suspected that the Professor had read none of the authors about whom he had such definite opinions. He used to say: "Nietzsche is the man. All the others are rubbish."

"And what about Heidegger, Professor?"

He would rub his face with both hands, the invariable prelude to one of his categorical statements: "A fake."

Marx?

"Completely washed-up."

Camus?

"A queer."

Professor Fortuna was always unshaven and, regardless of the season, wore an overcoat the colour of a wet rat. He is not an ugly man, but it was easier to believe in the sexual adventures he recounted ("I learned all I know in India") than to believe, as he claimed, that he could read Greek. He said that any day now he would hand over for publication the book he was writing, a response to *The Critique of Pure Reason*, which had the provisional title of *Anti Kant*. Although we knew almost nothing about his life, we were sure of two things: the book did not exist, and he had never read Kant. Or Nietzsche. But Dubin and I frequently involved him in our discussions, even when his table was far from ours and we had to shout so that he could hear us.

"What's your position on the comma, Professor?"

"I'm against them!"

The Professor's theory was that you could put a comma wherever you liked. The true test of a writer is the semi-colon, which, according to him, no-one had yet mastered. With the possible exception of Henry James, whom he clearly hadn't read either. A recurring topic of debate was: Can detective or spy fiction be good literature? I said it could, Dubin wasn't sure, and the Professor declared roundly that it was arrant rubbish. He reacted to my evidence to the contrary with dismissive noises. Graham Greene? Pffft! Rubem Fonseca? Ugh! Raymond Chandler? Hah! Once I asked him if he had bought a particular book by John le Carré.

"What for? I have enough toilet paper at home."

The only reason I didn't get up and hit him was because I couldn't. It was Saturday night, and I was already halfway down to the bottom of the pit.

But why am I telling you all this? Take it as a plea either for mercy or for punishment. An extenuating or perhaps aggravating factor for what is to come. My defence, or my condemnation. This is what I was before the first white envelope arrived. This is what we were. Garrulous but innocent members of the living dead. I swear we were innocent. Or take it merely as a description of the background into which, like a chameleon, I was gradually merging when the story began. First chapter, first scene, colon: a sulphurous swamp, a lake of lamentations, upon which, one day, a white envelope alighted like a lost bird.

It's all over now, what the stars ordained would happen has happened, and we are innocents no longer. Or, rather, we are not the same innocents. Nothing can be done or undone, all that's left is the story and our lingering guilt. Curse us, please. Be kind and curse us.

The first envelope arrived on a Tuesday. I was still suffering the effects of Monday's hangover and very nearly threw it in the bin unopened. However, there was something about the handwriting that made me hesitate. Something appealing, almost supplicatory, about those capital letters, written in a tremulous, childish hand, made me open the envelope. Inside were four sheets of paper held together between transparent covers by a spiral binding. On the first sheet, a title, "Ariadne", was written in ballpoint pen, with a little flower above the "i" instead of a dot. The one thing I never understood about this whole story was that little flower. If I *had* understood it, none of it would ever have happened, and we would all have been spared. Between the first and second sheet was a note folded in two. It was from someone signing themselves "A friend", who explained that the author of those sheets of paper did not know that they had been photocopied and sent to a publisher. They were the first pages of a diary or an autobiography or a confession. The "friend" asked that we read the text "kindly". If we were interested in publishing it, she would send us the rest of the book when it was ready. A "yes" from the publisher would help persuade the author to finish what she had begun with those few pages. "Please say Yes!" said the note in conclusion.

I read the first lines of that handwritten page.

> My father met a painter in Europe who was obcessed with Ariadne. I owe my name to a stranger's obcession. I sometimes think my whole life has been ruled by other people's obcessions. At least the obcession that will kill me will be mine alone because nothing is as self-indulgent or as solitary as suicide. But not yet not yet.

"Obsession" was spelt incorrectly, but that didn't make me throw the pages in the bin as I had with Corina's poems when she wrote "lusid" instead of "lucid". I continued reading. "Ariadne" was twenty-five. She would not commit suicide at once because "I need to close myself up gradually like someone closing up a house before setting off on a journey. Window by window room by room. My heart first." Only with her heart closed could she avenge herself for what they had done to her and to someone she called the "Secret Lover". To avenge herself on those who had destroyed everything: "Our past the living room in the old house with the candles burning on the floor the corner of the ruined garden where he said that if the moon smiled she would resemble me and I cried 'Are you calling me "Moonface"?!' and he kissed me on the mouth for the first time." Only with her heart closed could she exact a just revenge for what they had done to her father too: "The poor distracted man probably doesn't even know he's dead." In those first four pages there was no explanation as to who "they" were, the people on whom Ariadne would take her revenge before committing suicide. Nor what form her vengeance or suicide would take. The pages ended with her evoking "the house of the catalpa tree", home, I presumed, to the living room with the candles burning on the floor and the ruined garden where she and the Secret Lover met.

I found those four pages fascinating. Not because of their literary value – that smiling moon was a bit too much for me to stomach (well, I hadn't quite recovered from the weekend's drinking). I don't really know what it was I found so enchanting, which means that I cannot explain this whole story. It was like being dazzled, in the sense of being in the presence of a light that dissolves all shadows. It was a sudden incursion into the darkness in which I lived. Ariadne had invaded my mind along with the light emanating from her words. I imagined her so entirely and so intensely that my next feeling was an absurd twinge of jealousy for that Secret Lover. Or perhaps what attracted me was the imminent tragedy she described, my identification with a co-suicide-in-the-making. Or perhaps it was just the complete absence of commas.

I looked at the back of the envelope. The return address was a P.O. Box in the town of Frondosa.

Marcito's secretary is called Bela. She's a tall, buxom, blonde Italian with rosy cheeks. We work in the same room. Whenever Dubin came into the office, he would sing, "Bela, Bela Giovanella," and she would roll her eyes and sigh, weary of the effect she had on foolish men. In response to little Dubin's invitations to join him at some smart café in the country ("My dream is to possess you somewhere that serves seven different types of jam," he would say), she would suggest that he come back when he had grown up. Lovely Bela has a lover who is older than her, although we don't know what exactly goes on in Marcito's office when he calls her in and shuts the door. Whatever it is they do behind that door, they do it in silence.

Bela and I were alone on the afternoon the white envelope arrived and I asked her if she knew where Frondosa was.

"Frondosa, Frondosa . . . Hmmm, it's certainly nowhere near where I come from."

Until she was fifteen, lovely Bela had lived in an area in deepest Rio Grande do Sul that had been colonised by Italians. Dubin claimed to have erotic fantasies about the lovely Bela walking barefoot among the pigs. He dreamed about her muddy calves. He said he had a thing about the calves of adolescent country girls. He used to ask the lovely Bela if the parish priest used to sit her on his knee and stroke her calves – he wanted to know all the details. The lovely Bela was not amused.

"Túlio will know where Frondosa is," she said, pointing at the white envelope. Túlio is a salesman for the fertiliser factory owned by Marcito's uncle. He travels all over the state. He's the one who delivers the firm's almanac to the factory's customers. He was bound to know everything about Frondosa. "He'll be here tomorrow," said the lovely Bela, before returning to her copy of *Hello!* magazine.

Ariadne. With a little flower above the "i". Was it a fictitious name? Her father, whether fictitious or not, had chosen the name. How did the myth of Ariadne go now? She was the daughter of Minos, King of Crete. She fell in love with Theseus, to whom she gave a ball of thread so that he could find his way out of the Labyrinth once he had killed the Minotaur. Ariadne had stood at the entrance, holding the end of the thread for her lover. Now there was another Ariadne, whether fictitious or not, holding the end of a thread in a place called Frondosa. The other end of the thread was there before me. A tiny thread. A mere nothing. Just a P.O. Box number in an unknown town, on the back of a white envelope. A beginning.

2

"I THINK I'VE READ THAT PHRASE SOMEWHERE BEFORE," SAID Dubin.

"Which phrase?"

"'If the moon smiled she would resemble you.' And it wasn't on a lavatory wall either."

It was Wednesday. Dubin had arrived, given his usual greeting – "Bela, Bela Giovanella" – and read the four manuscript pages, having first perused the accompanying letter. His hunch was that the "friend" of the letter and the "Ariadne" of the text were one and the same. You could tell by the absence of commas in both documents. He liked the diary-cum-autobiography, though. The author was obviously a keen reader, despite the errors in punctuation and spelling. He didn't believe it had been written by a potential suicide. Not a real one anyway: "It's a fiction. Phoney literary despair. You get a lot of it in those small towns."

Dubin had invented a town in the *interior* called Santa Edwige dos Aflitos – St Edwige of the Afflicted – to sum up his affectionate scorn for anyone who did not live in the capital. Now and again, he would supply us with new information about the town, which had "the best carnival in the whole Piruiri valley", the Piruiri being a river he had also invented. Santa Edwige was the biggest producer of hay in Brazil, and every year they held a National Festival of Hay, known as the HayHoedown, during which the queen and the princesses of the harvest were chosen at dances held in the Clube Comercial, where, on the occasion of a rare appearance by Agnaldo Rayol, the prefect's wife had made a complete spectacle of herself by clinging to the singer's legs. According to Dubin, there was a local Academy of Letters with 127 members and a football team that was at the bottom of the state's bottom division and was awaiting the creation of another division so that it could be relegated still further. The local Academy of Letters would be full of Ariadnes like ours – perhaps a little older and less gifted – but no real suicides.

Túlio arrived and greeted us with his usual enthusiasm ("Gentlemen! *Signorina!*"), but this time I interrupted his swift passage through our room and into Marcito's office and asked if he could tell us anything about a town called Frondosa. He didn't even have to think. "Frondosa? Galotto."

"Galotto?"

"The Galotto factory. The owners of the factory own the town."

"Are they very powerful?"

"Powerful and rich. The most powerful company in the region."

"Where is Frondosa?"

"Have you got a map?"

I had. Túlio's finger hovered over one area of the map for a few seconds before finding the right place to land. There it was: Frondosa.

"Its a very pretty area, although the town's no great shakes. Apparently, it takes its name from a big, leafy tree that used to stand in the square."

Túlio is a burly fellow, nearly six foot six tall, with a pleasant, swarthy, rather Arabian face. He travels all over the state selling fertiliser and distributing our almanac, so he has contacts everywhere. Did he know anyone in Frondosa?

"Let's see . . . The people I have most to do with there are the staff at the agricultural cooperative. No, wait, I do know a Galotto."

"One of the owners of the factory?"

"No, the factory doesn't belong to the Galotto family anymore. They kept the name, but it's under different ownership now. The man who started the business was Aldo Galotto, a tinsmith. He passed it on to his son, whose name I forget now, but who made the business into a real force to be reckoned with. But *his* son wanted nothing to do with the business – he was a painter. He lived for a long time in Europe, where he mixed with all kinds of artists. The factory ended up in the hands of his son-in-law, Martelli, and the Galottos were left with nothing. I don't know how the Galotto fellow I know manages to live. I guess his sister gives him money. He's a nice fellow, a good talker, but an idle so-and-so. He spends all his time playing snooker. And he drinks like a fish."

"So the artist only had one son and one daughter?"

"I'm not sure. I think there's a younger brother too, or was. Something happened to him. I can't quite remember what . . . Or perhaps that was another member of the family. I don't recall."

"Do you know the sister's name?"

"The one who's married to Martelli? No, but I can find out. Why do you want to know all this?"

Dubin answered for me:

"We're looking for new authors."

Túlio undertook to find out the sister's name. It was unlikely she was *our* Ariadne. Only the reference to the artist father who had known other artists in Europe connected her to the Galotto family. And if she *was* our Ariadne, she would hardly be using her own name. We needed to investigate. First step: reply to the letter from the "friend". I wrote saying that we were very impressed by the sample she had sent us of Ariadne's work and would like to see more. It would help if she could give us more information about herself and about the author. If the rest of the book was as good as the sample, we would seriously consider publishing it, but we needed to know who we were dealing with. We would also require a photograph of Ariadne. For some reason, I signed the letter with a pseudonym: Agomar Peniche, Editorial Director. Second step: I went into Marcito's office, flung the four sheets of paper down on his desk and said: "*This* is good." He didn't even look at them. When he asked what they were, I told him and said they were worth investing in. This provoked a pained look.

"How much?"

"I don't know," I said. "I don't know how long it's going to be."

Marcito continued to suffer. "Will it sell?"

"I believe we will be launching a fine new writer who will bring prestige and critical acclaim to the publishing house. Or are we only interested in making money?"

"I don't know about you, but that's all I'm interested in."

"The story might be true, though. In which case it could turn out to be a *succès de scandale*."

Marcito dismissed me with a gesture, irritated less by my pushiness than by my French. I took this as a Yes.

That Friday, I decided to take the pages to the Bar do Espanhol to get Professor Fortuna's opinion. His theory was that literature, like stevedoring and Formula 1 racing, was not a suitable career for women. Whenever I cited examples of great women writers, he would shake his head and smile a demoniacal smile. According to him, the only thing women achieved with their literature was to drive themselves and those around them mad. He said women writers had ruined the lives of more men than prostitutes and gambling. He had serious doubts about the wisdom of teaching

25

women to write at all and advised strong corrective action at the first sign of literary ambitions in young girls. That's why we were surprised when he read the four pages and said, "Not bad."

"You mean you liked it, Professor?"

"As I said, it's not bad."

"Virginia Woolf or Madame Dely?"

"More like Ivona Gabor."

Dubin and I looked at each other. Ivona Gabor?

"Hungarian," the Professor said. "You wouldn't know her."

"What did she write?"

The Professor sighed and made a vague gesture. We could hardly expect him to summon up, just like that, the works of Ivona Gabor, which were, apparently, legion.

"Is she dead?"

"Oh, she died a long time ago, killed herself, but not without first sending her husband and her whole family mad. Yet another example of the imprudence of the indiscriminate teaching of literacy."

My letter to the P.O. Box in Frondosa had been sent on the Thursday. We reckoned that a reply, and possibly more pages, would arrive on the following Wednesday. All we could do was wait. We spent the rest of that Friday re-reading and discussing Ariadne's manuscript. Dubin even went so far as to take a pen from his pocket, but I stopped him before he could start spattering the text with commas. Could our Ariadne have anything to do with the story of the Galotto family in Frondosa? It would be a huge coincidence, but it was an attractive hypothesis. We sought more information about Frondosa from our immediate surroundings, namely, the other regulars at the Bar do Espanhol. Tavinho, who knows everything about football, the only subject that seems to interest him, told us that Frondosa had a football team, but for *futebol de salão*, Brazilian five-a-side. It was supported by some local industrialist whose name he had forgotten. Galotto? Yes, that was it! Did anyone else in the bar know anything about Frondoso? No-one. Most didn't even know the town existed. We only knew that the author's father had been to Europe, where he had met a painter obsessed with the mythical figure of Ariadne. Her father must be the artistic Galotto, who wanted nothing to do with the factory. This would make Ariadne, his daughter, Martelli's wife. And she had cheated on Martelli with the Secret Lover.

"Martelli found out and killed the lover."

"That's the story she's writing."

"The book will be her revenge."

Dubin rubbed his hands together gleefully. His fictitious Santa Edwige dos Aflitos had known only one crime of passion in its entire history, and that had been years ago. The affair had ended with a geography teacher being castrated and an heiress banished to a convent. The history of Frondosa promised far more. Always assuming, of course, that it wasn't just another fiction.

"De Chirico," Tavinho said suddenly.

We looked at him, surprised.

"What?"

"The painter obsessed with Ariadne. His name was De Chirico. He was a major influence on the Surrealists."

We stared at him, open-mouthed. How did Tavinho, who only ever talked about football, know that? He knew more too.

"De Chirico died in Rome."

"How do you know?"

"I support Lazio," Tavinho said, as if this explained everything. "I know all there is to know about Rome. Would you like me to list the names of all the Popes?"

We spent the rest of the evening speculating about Ariadne's manuscript and the real or imagined drama she would reveal to us. Only at midnight did I realise that I had drunk just one glass of *cachaça*. The "Inaugural Drink", I call it. Ariadne had so filled my mind that I had forgotten to drink and had gone no further than that first inaugural shot of rum. I arrived home sober. Black the dog looked at me, astonished, but said nothing.

3

THE BAR DO ESPANHOL HAS A DEVOTED CLIENTELE. THE MINOR poet and I go there every weekend. Professor Fortuna, I imagine, used to go there every day. Tavinho is always there. Indeed, we don't know what he does when he isn't propping up the bar, discussing football with someone. And there are a few other regulars too. And I had begun to notice a new and constant presence in the bar, a lugubrious young man with deep-set eyes who sat alone at a table, his back against the wall, and who would stare, without blinking, in my direction, and linger over an endless glass of mineral water. We had tried to draw him into our investigation – "Do you know Frondosa?" – but he said nothing and temporarily averted his gaze, before once again fixing me with that intense, reptilian stare.

On the following Friday, I arrived at the bar with the reply I had received from the "friend" during the week, addressed to Agomar

Peniche. Who was Agomar Peniche? It took me a while to remember that I myself had invented the pseudonym. The letter arrived without the promised next instalment of Ariadne's book. The "friend" thanked us for our interest and explained that she was having difficulty gaining access to the text, because Ariadne's activities were "restricted" and she had to write in secret. These restrictions were such that if found out she risked death.

"Wow!" Tavinho exclaimed.

I read the rest of the letter, in which the "friend" swore that she would send more of the story soon, urging us to be as "discrete" as possible, because no-one in Frondosa must know that Ariadne was writing a book. I kept the best until last. When I took the photograph of Ariadne out of the envelope, there was a chorus of "Wow!"s. The Spaniard even abandoned his cash register to find out what could have provoked such enthusiasm.

Ariadne at a dance. White dress, long, blonde hair falling onto bare shoulders. Ariadne smiling at the camera. There was a touch of irony in that smile, an irony directed at the situation in which she found herself being photographed and at her own youthful glow. The smile of someone who knows she is the prettiest girl at the party, the prettiest girl in town, but who attaches no importance to it. According to Dubin – basing himself on the social calendar of Santa Edwige dos Aflitos – the occasion must have been a debutantes' ball, which meant that Ariadne would have been only fifteen when the photo was taken. Her smile, though, was older.

It was the smile of someone who has already lived more than her smile. And it justified the words used by the "Secret Lover": if the moon smiled, that is exactly what it would look like. The expression in her eyes, though, was sad; no, not sad, but distant, absent. There was a sense of loss in them. Something had come to an end in the life of that adolescent – apart from childhood, that is. Or perhaps I was simply seeing what I wanted to see. I needed that sad smile and that sense of loss in order, finally, to fall in love. The photograph had a stamp on the back – *Fotos Mazaretto* – and an address in Rua Voluntários da Pátria. Dubin used to describe how the debutantes' balls that took place in Santa Edwige dos Aflitos, organised by Fanfan le Tulipe, the local society columnist, were marred each year by the boys drinking too much whisky and guaraná just so as to pluck up enough courage to ask the girls to dance, but throwing up over their dinner jackets before they could do so. The girls, though, were lovely, ripe for the picking, semi-virgins every one. I had to wrench the photo of Ariadne from Dubin's hands, for he had, one day, confessed to me his other fetish, apart from girls' calves, which was to slow-dance with just such a nymph at some mythical ball in one of those small provincial towns, rest his head on her pubescent breast and have her lean down and whisper in his ear: "Are you following the latest TV soap?" Ecstasy! Ecstasy! But he wouldn't be doing that with Ariadne. Not with my Ariadne. I put the photograph back in the envelope.

*

Tavinho was impressed.

"What does she mean about Ariadne 'risking death'?"

In his efforts to dredge up De Chirico's name, he had not heard us explaining what we knew, or imagined, about Ariadne, that she was married to a Frondosa tycoon, whom she had betrayed with a lover. That something had happened to the lover, who had, perhaps, been killed. That Ariadne had started writing a diary or an autobiography or a confession, to tell the world what had happened.

"Or hasn't happened," said Professor Fortuna, for whom Ariadne's text was clearly a fiction.

He agreed with Dubin: the letter had been written by Ariadne herself, who was busily inventing the rest of the story now that she had learned there was a publisher interested. "Risking death" was merely a melodramatic phrase used to ensure our continuing interest. But Dubin was beginning to think that the story might be true. After all, we had a photo now. We had seen the protagonist's face.

I had no doubts at all. I needed the story to be true. I believed that Ariadne was at real risk of dying, that my beloved wrote in secret, perhaps under the bedclothes by torchlight, afraid that he might see her and kill her as he had killed the "Secret Lover". "He" being her husband. I already had a clear image of him, composed entirely of my own personal prejudices. One of those brash young businessmen, arrogant, macho, insensitive and reactionary. He probably had a mistress too, and beat his wife. Yes, he beat my beloved. Whatever revenge Ariadne was concocting before taking her own life, he deserved it. I hated him.

The second letter from the "friend" was as well written as the first, except that she clearly didn't know the difference between "discreet" and "discrete". She did not, however, answer my questions.

She revealed neither her name nor Ariadne's true identity. I decided to leave things as they were and not to write again. Agomar Peniche would wait. We would all wait for the next instalment of the story of Ariadne and her revenge. That night, I surprised myself again. I had ordered my usual Inaugural Drink, followed by a beer and another *cachaça* – still beneath the reptilian gaze of the strange young man – and went home sober. Only when I was lying next to Julinha, who received me with a grunt, unlike Black the dog, who smiled and said, "Hello there, pal," only then did I understand my reason for arriving home still conscious. I slipped out from between the sheets and took the envelope from my inside jacket pocket. I removed the photograph and carried it back to bed with me. When Julinha, bothered by the light, shifted ponderously beside me and seemed about to wake up, I put the bedside lamp under the covers, as I did when I was a child and my mother used to tell me to turn out the light when what I really wanted was to continue reading. Now all I wanted was to go on looking at the photograph of Ariadne. I don't know how long I spent gazing at her. I think I fell asleep with the photo lying on my chest. Ariadne. Fifteen years old. Long, blonde hair falling onto bare shoulders.

The following week, Túlio turned up at the office with some news. He had been doing some investigating and had discovered that Martelli's wife was called – can you imagine? – Ariadne! So the author's name wasn't a pseudonym. We had guessed correctly: our Ariadne was the artistic Galotto's daughter and Martelli's wife. Not only was her story true, she hadn't even bothered to disguise her name. The person holding the end of the thread that would lead us to Frondosa was a real-life Ariadne. In the meantime, I had been carrying out my own investigations with the reluctant help of the beautiful Bela, whose response to any interruption of her magazine-reading was a scowl and a demand for extra pay. I had found out a few things about Frondosa and about the history of the Galotto factory since its foundation. Frondosa had fewer than 50,000 inhabitants. It was located in an area that grew soya and wheat, but the Galotto factory was responsible, directly and indirectly, for almost half the jobs in the region. The town was right in the middle of a geological anomaly, a kind of crater that had led people to speculate that it had once been the site of a volcano. There were two Martelli brothers, Fabrizio and Franco. One of them had been or still was the town's mayor. One of them was Ariadne's husband. But which? Túlio didn't know. He only knew that Mayor Martelli had ordered the leafy tree in the middle of the main square to be cut down and replaced by a large concrete circle.

"I have to go to Frondosa later this month. So if you need anything . . ." he said.

Friday came and went, but no new white envelope arrived from Frondosa. No letter from the "friend", and no new instalment of the story. On our way to the Bar do Espanhol, Dubin and I speculated about what might have happened.

"Perhaps Martelli found out what she was doing and killed her, or at least confiscated her pen," Dubin suggested.

"Bastard!" I said, surprising him with my vehemence.

For Professor Fortuna the explanation was obvious: the author was taking pains to write a second chapter as good as the first. Or perhaps there was more than one author. Perhaps it was a group of women with nothing else to do, writing a first-person narrative just for the fun of it. Perhaps none of them was Ariadne, whose love affair would be common knowledge in the town and had merely served as inspiration for the false diary. Perhaps it was all just gossip. Well written, but gossip nonetheless. Tavinho had a more practical explanation for the silence from Frondosa: "Perhaps the post was delayed."

I had the photo of Ariadne in my pocket. I placed it on the table, beside my Inaugural Drink. How old would she be now? Twenty-five, she had said in that first chapter. And what if Professor Fortuna was right and the manuscript was a joke, a hoax, and that photograph was of some young woman from Frondosa, chosen purely so that her beauty would further provoke the curiosity of Agomar Trapiche, or Peniche, or whatever stupid name I had given myself? And what if my obsession of recent days was about nothing at all and what if, at the end of the thread that would lead me to Ariadne so that I could save her or she could save me, there was also nothing? A joke, a confidence trick? But I loved Ariadne. Even if she didn't exist, I loved her. And I hated Martelli. Which of the two brothers was the murderous husband? Fabrizio or Franco? I hated them both! I downed the Inaugural Drink in one and ordered a beer, too. This would be followed by another *cachaça*, another beer, another *cachaça* . . . My toboggan into blessed oblivion. The last thing I remember hearing was Dubin challenging the Professor to give him one, just one, title of a book by Ivona Gabor, and the Professor saying something like *Scapinski madjar oluvova* and apologising for his rather rusty Hungarian, one of the seven languages he spoke.

I have no memory of what happened next, but Dubin tells me that I suddenly got up from my chair, staggered over to the table occupied by the stranger who never stopped staring at me and demanded: "Whassaproblem?" And that the stranger pointed two fingers in my direction and said, "Zap!", as if blasting me to pieces with a ray-gun. And then I collapsed onto the floor.

4

I WAS STILL IN PIECES ON MONDAY. A BLACK HANGOVER, THE
worst in many years. A hard, dry ball of faecal matter had lost its
way and was threatening to emerge from my mouth. A porcupine
had taken the place of my brain. I picked up the four envelopes
brought by the postman that morning, threw them into the
wastepaper bin and gave it a kick. Then I remembered that I
needed the addresses so I could write and tell all the authors to
shove their manuscripts up their arses. Only when I retrieved
them did I realise that one of the envelopes was white, had been
posted in Frondosa and was addressed in that same tremulous
hand. Inside, between transparent plastic covers, were ten spiral-
bound manuscript pages. There was no letter from the "friend",
only Ariadne's photocopied text with the little flower above

the "i". The second chapter. It began thus: "Dying is an art like everything else."

I must have spent five minutes just staring at that first sentence. Not because my porcupine-brain refused to work, but because the sentence paralysed me. A single sentence at the top of the page, like an epigraph. "Dying is an art like everything else." What did that mean? Was she going to orchestrate her own death, design it, treat it like a work of art, perform it like a play? Or was she talking about someone else, another dead person? When I managed to detach myself from that first sentence, I realised that she was writing about her father. About her memories of her father. His large hands that smelled of turpentine, stroking her hair as she sat on his lap on his reclining chair. His name for her. "Figliola". Her clearest recollections were also the most distant: she a little child on his lap, he enormous in his equally enormous reclining chair, with his legs sticking out. The feeling she had of being on board a ship whenever she climbed onto her father's chair. That's what he used to say: "Figliola come on board." And she would close her eyes, snug on his lap, and imagine the ship sailing the high seas. Just the two of them, sailing, sailing . . . Where? He would say, "Full steam ahead for the Eastern star. Hold hard for the Eastern star." All ten pages were about her father. About the journeys he had made before he got married. About the art courses he took in Paris and in Rome, where he had met De Chirico and other painters, and the year he spent in Spain:

When I married my father wanted to treat us to a whole month in Europe but my husband wouldn't accept. He said that he needed to start work at once since marrying me made him the youngest shareholder in the business. Later he told me that he hadn't accepted because my father needed to stop squandering money. A month in Europe would be very expensive. Our honeymoon consisted of five days by the sea in Punta del Este. "The wrong direction" my father whispered in my ear when we set out. "The Eastern star is the other way."

Her father never returned to Europe. The factory was bankrupt. A few years later, there was a meeting at which her husband and his brother, who had acquired a majority share in the company, removed her father from the board. "The day of the long knives," according to Ariadne. She remembered her father arriving at her house after the meeting, barely able to speak, opening his arms to embrace her and saying, "Figliola figliola . . ." She had been frightened, not knowing what had happened to him. He was so absent-minded, perhaps he had fallen over in the street. She said "Are you hurt?" and looked for signs of bleeding. A few weeks later, he was dead. "But they'll pay," Ariadne wrote:

> They'll pay for the death of my father they'll pay for
> what they did to the Secret Lover they'll pay for what

they did to me. I've died several times over the years
but this time I'm going to leave a will. This is my will.
Like the cat I have nine times to die. Time to perfect
the art.

That same day, I wrote a letter to the "friend", addressed to the
P.O. Box in Frondosa. I said that we were definitely interested
in Ariadne's book. That the second chapter confirmed the work's
literary quality, although it might need a little tweaking. That we
should meet to draw up a contract. That it was simply a matter of
naming a date and someone from the publishing house would
come out to Frondosa to talk to Ariadne. Or with the "friend".

That same Wednesday, I waited until Dubin had finished reading
the ten new pages before announcing:

"We're going to put a man in."

Dubin didn't understand. It was the kind of expression you
find in spy thrillers.

"We need someone in Frondosa."

"What do you mean, 'someone'?"

"Someone to investigate this story. To get in touch with
Ariadne or with her 'friend' or with whoever can give us information about her and her family, and about the Martelli brothers. To
find out who it is we're dealing with if we do decide to publish the
book. And, ultimately, to avoid a trial. Or a murder. Or a suicide."

"And who would that someone be?"

"You."

"Me?!"

"You will be the company's representative. Túlio will be going to Frondosa at the end of the month. You can hitch a ride with him."

"Why not you?"

I didn't answer. Why not me? Why didn't I go to Frondosa? Absurdly, I thought: because my meeting with Ariadne has to be the story's climax, the Labyrinth's end. Because I am going to save her, and save myself, and until then, it's all prologue. Because ever since that first white envelope alighted on my life, I have been as if bewitched, and arriving in Frondosa too soon would break the spell. Because until I meet Ariadne, my role is to control the story from a distance and make sure we don't lose the thread. I am, after all, the editor.

"No, *you* must go, Dubin."

The "friend's" answer was not long in coming. She was in a state of panic. "Please don't come to Frondosa! Don't send anyone! No-one here must know that Ariadne is writing the book. It would be a scandal. Wait until she has finished. Then we can decide what to do." Finally, in capital letters, underlined, she wrote: "DON'T COME!"

We met in the Bar do Espanhol to launch what I called "Operation Theseus" in homage to the first man to be bewitched by Ariadne,

41

the first to follow the thread. Professor Fortuna managed to overcome his horror of physical contact and join us in our plotting, squeezed in between Dubin and Tavinho, although he was still sceptical, believing the book to be a lie. A con, a swindle. The last letter from the "friend", imploring me not to let anyone from the publishing house go to Frondosa, had only increased his suspicions. If they didn't want anyone to know that Ariadne was writing a book, if Ariadne was endangering her own life by writing a book, why didn't she use a pseudonym? Why had she used her own name as the title? And yet it was the unbelieving Professor who thumped the table, impatient to get to work. What was the plan?

"Operation Theseus consists of our sending a man into Frondosa," I announced rather solemnly.

Dubin didn't really care anymore if the story was fictitious or not. We had to find out what was at the other end of that thread. Ariadne, whether true or false, had bewitched him too. And he was ready for his mission. He had even chosen a code name.

"Nick?!"

"Yes, Nick. Nick Stradivarius."

"Look, Dubin, this is a serious business," I protested. "Someone's life may be at risk."

"I know it's serious. I'm being serious."

It had become clear – after the last terrified letter from the "friend" – that our agent would have to enter Frondosa in disguise and carry out his investigations under cover. No-one must know what Dubin was trying to find out, far less his connection with the publishing house. We would ask Túlio to introduce him around the town as . . . as . . .

"As a film producer," Dubin suggested. "I'm there looking for locations for a film. I could even approach the Martelli brothers to ask them to sponsor the film, in exchange for advertising their businesses."

"I'm not sure."

"No, think about it. I could get myself invited to the Martelli household and meet Ariadne. I could go anywhere I wanted, enter every house, all on the pretext of looking for suitable locations. It's perfect. I'm going to start practising my accent."

"You're going to have an accent?"

"Nick Stradivarius needs an accent. I was thinking of something vaguely Italian or—"

"Just one question," I said, interrupting him. "Why would an Italian film producer arrive in Frondosa in the company of a fertiliser salesman?"

"And I have just one question for you," Dubin said.

"What's that?"

"Who's going to finance all this? Because I'm going to need some props. Not to mention a pair of Italian shoes and, at the very least, a scarf and a pipe. And a daily allowance for food and accommodation. Where's the money going to come from?"

"I'll speak to Marcito."

"And there's no problem about arriving in Frondosa with a

fertiliser salesman, *caro mio*," Dubin went on, already trying out his Italian accent. "The fertiliser factory has a role in the film too. We'll say that it was Túlio, who knows the whole state, who recommended the picturesque town of Frondosa as a film location."

Dubin could already imagine himself choosing a cast of extras from among the adolescent girls of Frondosa, feeling their calves and explaining what a very important part they would play in the plot. Professor Fortuna interrupted Dubin's ramblings with another rap on the table and suggested that we focus on practical matters. For example: How long would our man remain under cover in Frondosa? Would he send messages or just report back when he returned at the end of the mission? How would we communicate with him? I noticed a certain resentment on the part of Professor Fortuna because we had chosen Dubin as our inside man. We had never before seen the Professor so excited. I realised that, for all his grumpy scepticism, he, too, had been bewitched by Ariadne. The Spaniard had posted himself beside our table so as not to miss the conversation. The lugubrious fellow with the reptilian gaze moved closer so that he could eavesdrop on our plans. Ariadne's thread had hooked us all.

Tavinho was concerned about the cover story we would have to come up with for Nick Stradivarius, or, as it is known in the world of espionage, his "legend", a spy's false identity. For example, what if someone were to ask him what films he had produced?

44

Dubin had an answer ready: "Nicola Stradivarius is unknown outside of Europe. His films are never shown in Brazil, far less in Frondosa, which probably doesn't even have a cinema."

"But it has a video shop."

It took us a while to realise that this last remark had come from the lugubrious fellow at the next table. His contribution to the conspiracy was rejected by Dubin, who believed that no-one in Frondosa would go to the trouble of checking out Nick Stradivarius's credentials. According to Dubin, these provincial towns welcome world celebrities and don't ask too many questions. At least that was how it was in Santa Edwige dos Aflitos, where a supposed great-niece of Mussolini and the supposed inventor of the laser beam lived quite happily without ever having to prove that they were who they said they were.

To my surprise, Marcito did not laugh at my request. Money to finance Dubin's incursion into Frondosa to investigate the origins of a book that was arriving at the office in instalments? How much did I want? I hadn't expected him to agree, so I had to come up with a figure on the spot. Enough for three or four nights in a hotel, plus food. "Done," he said. "I'll write you a cheque." I could only conclude that this unexpected burst of good will had something to do with his admiration for Simenon. Inspector Maigret would approve. Or perhaps, mysteriously, Marcito was as bewitched as the rest of us.

5

DUBIN'S PORTUGUESE CLASSES WERE HIGHLY THEATRICAL. HE
used to don an eye-patch to teach his students about Camões
and the pronoun, and wrap a bath towel around himself as a make-
shift toga when discussing Latin prefixes. And in his lesson on
clauses with no apparent subject, he would play the hidden subject
as a ghost, in a story full of creaking doors and sombre music
produced by the narrator himself. This was why his students took
it completely in their stride when he started speaking with an
Italian accent and gesticulating a lot. That was what they had come
to expect from their teacher, or, rather, their *professore*, as he now
insisted on being called. He was getting into the role of Nick
Stradivarius while he waited for Túlio to decide on the date of
his next visit to Frondosa.

In the bar, Tavinho, concerned that Operation Theseus should be a success, helped Dubin rehearse his legend, just in case he should be interrogated.

"Stradivarius. . . What relation are you to the violin?"

"A distant cousin."

"Which Italian actresses have you worked with?"

"Nicoletta Costabrava, Anna Maria Moffato, Gina Girardello, to whom I was also married, Sandra Corfu . . ." The names had to be false ones, to lessen the risk of being unmasked. Should anyone ask.

We asked Túlio to draw us a map of Frondosa. He didn't know the town well and so drew a very rudimentary plan, marking the few places he could remember. The agricultural cooperative. The main square, where a vast concrete circle had replaced the ancient tree from which the town took its name – the work of Mayor Martelli. And in the square, the hotel where Túlio usually stayed when he spent the night in Frondosa. Beside the hotel was the bar where he had met the Galotto who did nothing but drink and play snooker.

"Is that the best hotel in town?"

"It's the oldest. It's one of those places where, at the end of the day, they put out chairs for the guests so they can watch the comings and goings in the square. There's a more modern one too, where people doing business with the Galotto factory stay, but I don't know where that is. It's not in the square."

"And the factory?"

"There are two units outside the town, an older one and a newer one. They have a showroom in the pedestrian precinct, which is here, just off the square, in Rua Voluntários da Pátria."

"And the club?"

"That's here, on the other side of the square. And the town hall is here. It's the only one of the town's older buildings that has been preserved. Oh, and the church is here."

And what about the Martellis' house? Túlio had no idea. A house with a catalpa tree outside? No, he'd never seen one like that.

The plan was for Túlio to introduce Nick Stradivarius to the town. They could start with a visit to the town hall, where he would be presented as a producer scouting locations for a multinational film involving Brazilian and European actors and the participation of the local population. If Frondosa was chosen, it would gain international fame. That would be good for local tourism and for businesses based in the town.

"What kind of film is it?" Tavinho asked, deep in his role as instructor to our man inside.

Dubin did not hesitate: "An action-packed romantic drama full of violent passions and shapely female calves. Based on a story by the Hungarian writer Ivona Gabor. Adapted for Rio Grande do Sul, of course."

Professor Fortuna briskly rubbed both sides of his nose as if he were about to say something, but instead remained silent

49

and impervious. As Dubin rehearsed his lessons, the Professor watched stony-faced, even more stony-faced than usual.

I asked Túlio if there was a traditional meeting place in the town.

"The bar next door to the hotel is where the older people tend to meet. The young congregate in the bars in the pedestrian precinct."

We decided that the first thing Dubin should do was get into conversation with the Galotto who spent all day in the bar, gain his confidence and draw him out about his family, the Martelli brothers, the factory and Ariadne. According to Túlio, it wasn't difficult to get Galotto to talk. The difficulty, after a few brandies, was understanding what he was saying.

The lugubrious fellow with the deep-set eyes had, by then, joined our conspiracy. He made suggestions as to how Dubin should carry out his investigations in Frondosa, he pored over the map of the town and chatted to me about the operation. Especially about the nature of the contract we would draw up with Ariadne if we published her book, and about the company's policy regarding royalties in general. It did not take me long to realise that this lugubrious fellow was none other than Fulvio Edmar, the author with whom I had exchanged insulting letters about the unpaid royalties on *Astrology and Love*. At least he was speaking to me, instead of replacing my tonsils with my testicles, as he had threatened to do in one letter. Or blowing me to smithereens with an imaginary ray-gun. Nonetheless, I took care never to turn my back on him.

On the same day that Dubin and Túlio set off in the car for Frondosa –with Dubin sporting his mother's silk scarf and feeling very excited to be visiting a real-life Santa Edwige dos Aflitos, and with Túlio somewhat concerned that our adventure might damage the sales of fertiliser and tarnish his good name in Frondosa – another white envelope arrived. The third chapter.

It was about Ariadne's mother, whom she compared, initially, with the moon. The moon again. This time, though, it was a threatening, pitiless moon: "The moon was my mother. She wasn't sweet like Mary. Her blue garments unloosed small bats and owls." A witch of a moon, then. The opposite of the sweet Virgin with her starry mantle, "the protecting sky of all the children in the world". This malevolent moon had cast a shadow over Ariadne from the time she was thirteen. She was her father's favourite. Bats and owls flew out of her mother's sneering mouth as she accused her of trying to seduce her own father, of wanting her father all to herself, his beloved "figliola". In vain did she weep and implore her mother to love her too. Her mother wouldn't listen, the moon moved on. And Ariadne's mother died without ever forgiving her. Her mother and father had married in Frondosa, then departed on a prolonged honeymoon in Europe. By the time they returned, her mother was pregnant with their first child. Two years later, Ariadne had been born, and a year and a half after that, her younger brother. Ariadne's memory of her mother then was of a woman who never smiled, who patiently put up with her artist husband's "eccentricities" and distractions and did her best to be the practical one of the family: "She it was who, in order to pay off my father's debts decided to sell the house of the catalpa tree where my brothers and I had been brought up." She was affectionate with her three children, but that all changed when Ariadne turned thirteen: "It was as if my puberty were a direct challenge to her an unexpected attack against which she needed to defend herself." Her mother had died before her husband, and before Ariadne's marriage:

> At the hospital I spent all day at her bedside. In her final days she only opened her eyes once. She looked around the room then fixed her gaze on my face. I smiled at her and she immediately closed her eyes. It was almost comical if anything can be comical in the presence of death. It was as if we had passed each other in the street and she had turned away pretending she hadn't seen me. After she died I started going to church. I became a devotee of the Virgin Mary with an intensity that sometimes frightened even me. I realised that I was simply waiting for that first moon to disappear from my life in order to be adopted by this other moon. The sweet moon. The forgiving moon.

And it was while seated on a pew in the church in the main square in Frondosa, after her mother's death, that the Secret Lover had whispered in her ear that the house of the catalpa tree was empty. Abandoned and crumbling. And he suggested that they go and see it. She hesitated. She had a premonition, a bad feeling. Not quite understanding her own words, she said, "That would be like profaning the past."

But he insisted. He said he knew how to get into the house. He confessed that he sometimes slept there. She needed to go back, one last time, before they pulled it down to make way for a new building. The catalpa tree was still there. The catalpa tree was in flower. She needed to go back, if only to show solidarity with the flowering catalpa.

In what had once been the mansion's grand reception room, a few white candles were stuck to the floor with their own wax. The Secret Lover had filled the room with candles. He showed her where he slept, in one corner, on a crumpled sheet. She asked him why. She said it wasn't right to invade the past like that, she asked what he was looking for in the empty house, what it brought back to him. And he answered, "You." He saw her everywhere in the house, he said. As a child, running down the stairs. As an adolescent, slowly descending the same stairs, like a princess in a white dress, dressed for the debutantes' ball at the club. As a child again, at the piano, getting annoyed with herself when she played a wrong note and hammering away at the right one to fix it in her head. He saw her in the glow from every candle, in the flickering shadows on the walls. She smiled, but still with that bad feeling tightening her throat.

"I'm not that person anymore."

"Here in this house you are. You are all those people."

Taking her hand, he led her into the ruined garden, lit by the full moon. She smiled to see that scene, at once poignant and artificial; the luminous blue of the stone lions and the cracked flagstones reminded her of a badly painted backdrop like the one she had seen once at an opera in the Teatro La Fenice in Venice. She smiled at the Secret Lover, trying to persuade herself that none of this was happening.

And he said, "If the moon smiled she would resemble you."

"Are you calling me 'Moonface'?"

And then he had kissed her on the mouth, and she had let herself be kissed, thinking: Now we *are* profaning something.

That night, Dubin phoned my house from his hotel room in Frondosa to deliver his first report. Operation Theseus had got off to a bad start. The car journey had been long but uneventful; however, as soon as he got out of the car and set foot on the pavement outside the hotel, Dubin had heard a female voice exclaim, "Mr Dubin!" It was an ex-student of his who lived in Frondosa and happened to be passing at that exact moment, thus destroying, in a matter of seconds, the legend we had so painstakingly constructed for Nick Stradivarius. Dubin immediately had to come up with another legend to explain to the girl, called Paula, just what he was doing in town.

"I'm doing a sociological study on how family-owned businesses in provincial towns in Rio Grande do Sul pass from generation to generation."

"Don't you teach Portuguese anymore?"

"Oh yes, but you know how it is. One has to turn one's hand to . . ."

"I bet you've come to study the Galotto factory, am I right?"

"You are. Do you know anything about the Galotto family?"

"Only what everyone knows. Our newspaper is running a campaign against the mayor, Fabrizio Martelli. He's one of the brothers who now own the Galotto factory. Just look at what he did."

Paula had pointed to the square outside the hotel. She explained that the tree that gave the town its name had once stood where now there was nothing but a large concrete circle. The mayor had ordered the tree to be cut down. He was standing for re-election and her newspaper was opposing him. The editorial line was that the mayor had concrete for brains.

"So you're a journalist?"

"Sort of. I help my father, who owns the paper."

Dubin described Paula as "on the chubby side, but very tasty", even though he had not been able to examine her calves, and even though he suspected she might be intelligent. They had arranged to meet the following day so that she could tell him what she knew about the change in ownership of the Galotto factory. Túlio had then looked for the Galotto who usually drank in the bar next door to the hotel, but failed to find him. That conversation would also have to wait until the following day. Operation Theseus, with a slight emergency change to the script, was launched. And the Italian film producer Nick Stradivarius was dead and buried, along with his accent and his silk scarf, even before he had begun to exist.

I asked Dubin for his first impression of Frondosa.

"I reckon it's a place where you either lose your soul completely or become a saint."

A phrase from the chapter Ariadne had written about her mother and the moon had stayed in my head, like a musical refrain one can't shake off. "The moon drags the sea after it like a dark crime." What shadows had that malevolent moon cast on my poor Ariadne's soul? That was the sadness I had seen in her lost gaze in the photograph. And what dark crime had taken place among the ruins of that moonlit garden?

6

PROFESSOR FORTUNA SHOOK HIS HEAD WHEN HE HEARD about Dubin's phone call and his initial report on Operation Theseus. He felt it had been a mistake to send Dubin, who wasn't up to such a serious mission. Besides, Dubin would only be staying in Frondosa for a few days. He had to be back at his teaching post on the Monday, and so he wouldn't have time to learn anything of any substance. He was a short-term spy, another mistake. I didn't argue with the Professor. I went home early and sober, despite it being a Friday, and to the complete bewilderment of Black the dog, who had already given up trying to understand these changes in my routine. I saw in his eyes what he was trying to say: "I just don't understand you anymore, my friend." I had agreed with Dubin that he would phone me again that night. I needed to be at home in order to receive his report. I was, after all, head of operations. Black would simply have to get used to my new responsibilities.

*

The phone didn't ring until much later, at midnight. Dubin had just got back to his hotel and, he said, I would never guess where he had been. To supper at Paula's house, at the house of Paula's father, Afonso, the owner of the newspaper. He started telling me what he had learned.

"The story of the newspaper is just amazing," Dubin said. "The man—"

I interrupted him. "Did you manage to speak to the drunken Galotto?"

"No. He hasn't been seen at the bar. He must have checked in at a clinic to get dried out. But let me tell you about the newspaper. It's the only one in the region. They publish eight pages, six days a week. And they're campaigning against Fabrizio Martelli's re-election as mayor. He's the one who cut down the tree in the main square. The Martelli brothers own the Galotto factory and therefore the town as well. I asked how it was that the town's only newspaper could be so independent and even oppose the Martelli brothers. Afonso told me the most amazing story. Listen . . ."

Dubin always used to say that the real celebrities in places like Santa Edwige dos Aflitos are the local eccentrics. They are given protected status as part of a town's heritage and treated with the same deference that certain primitive tribes accord their mad people, whom they believe to have been touched by the gods. The municipal madman of Santa Edwige dos Aflitos was Zé Bragueta, who spent all his time whipping open his overcoat in front of young girls to reveal his unzipped fly, out of which protruded, not his penis, but a small replica of the national flag. He also made endless speeches inveighing against the Pope and the Americans. The most famous eccentric in Frondosa was Diamantino Reis, known by everyone there as The Man Who Bet on Uruguay. In the 1950 World Cup, Diamantino had bet every penny he had on Uruguay beating Brazil in the final. His madness had two consequences. At a single stroke he became both a millionaire and a pariah, accused by the townsfolk of being a traitor to his country. He acquired the scornful nickname of "The Uruguayan". He put his winnings to good use and further increased his fortune, thus displeasing the local population still more. For years, Diamantino could not go out into the street without being insulted ("Filthy Uruguayan!") and threatened. He was now eighty-four. He had spent almost sixty years trying to redeem himself for having bet on Uruguay and got rich. He gave interest-free loans to anyone who asked, he made donations to all the local charities. And he was always on the lookout for popular causes he could support. He lent money to Loló, who ran the town brothel behind the cemetery, when the brothel faced closure due to competition from the new motels springing up all over the region, and he backed Afonso's newspaper, the *Frondosa Folio*, in its opposition to Mayor Fabrizio Martelli, an opposition that only intensified when the mayor cut down the ancient tree that had given both the town and the newspaper their name, and replaced it with that hideous circle of bare concrete. And thus, gradually, Diamantino had managed to gain the status of a venerable eccentric like Zé Bragueta. He was almost forgiven. Some still refused to serve him or to frequent his restaurant, Galeteria Brasil, which was decorated entirely in the national colours of green and yellow, with photos on the walls of Brazil's line-up for the 1950 World Cup, but many of the youth of Frondosa didn't even know the unfortunate origin of his wealth, nor why he was called "The Uruguayan" when he clearly wasn't from Uruguay. The older generation had convinced themselves that his crazy bet on Uruguay only proved that he had been touched by the gods. And they all speculated on how much money he would leave when he died. For Dubin, Frondosa was proving to be a Santa Edwige dos Aflitos that not even he could have dreamed up.

I asked Dubin what he had found out about the Galotto family, the Martelli brothers and Ariadne. Paula and her father knew all about the coup staged by the Martelli brothers to remove the Galotto family from the board at the factory. Paula had been friends with Ariadne. At one time, they had even exchanged poetry books – that is, when Ariadne was in Frondosa, for she spent long periods in Europe. Then Paula had gone to Porto Alegre to study and lost touch with her friend, although she had attended Ariadne's wedding in the church in the square. The wedding had been a major event in the town. The joke doing the rounds was that old Galotto had squandered all the money he no longer had on what

Lúcio Flávio, the *Frondosa Folio*'s society columnist, described as "the apotheotic lavishness" of the ceremony and the reception afterwards at the club. Had Franco married Ariadne as a shortcut to taking over the Galotto factory? Paula didn't think so. People even thought the opposite, that Ariadne had married Franco so that he could help her father save the factory. And yet they seemed very much in love. Ariadne stood by her husband after the coup at the factory, and there was no sign of any disagreement between them, not even after her father's death, which had been caused – or so everyone said – by the shock of losing power to the Martelli brothers. Did Paula still see Ariadne? No. Ariadne rarely appeared in public. She rarely left the house. It was said that her husband was over-protective.

"When I think about it," Paula said to Dubin, "the last time I spoke to Ariadne, apart from congratulating her on her wedding day, was when she returned from a trip to Europe with her father and brought me a book of poems in English. I still have it some-where. With an inscription from her."

Struggling to keep his questions purely sociological and investi-gative in tone, Dubin asked what Paula and her father could tell him about the rest of the Galotto family. Ariadne had two brothers, didn't she?

"Yes. An older and a younger one."

"And what do they do?"

"The older brother doesn't do anything apart from drink. He's a hopeless case really, a permanent fixture in the bar next door to your hotel. No-one knows what exactly he lives on."

"And the younger one?"

"He vanished. He must have left Frondosa. No-one has seen him in ages." Paula went on to say that Ariadne's younger brother was the son most like their father. Airy-fairy. From another galaxy. A romantic. "He has dreamy eyes like yours, Mr Dubin," she said, smiling.

And Dubin told me that he had, by then, had time to examine Paula's calf muscles, and found that they more than made up for the fact that Paula could speak English and French and liked poetry. Something else gave him hope that she wasn't an "intellectual", which was a synonym in the Bar do Espanhol for a complicated type of woman best avoided. He had seen a copy of Fulvio Edmar's *Astrology and Love* on a shelf in her house. If Paula read *Astrology and Love*, then she was someone with whom Dubin could fall in love. If he discovered that she had underlined certain sections of the book, he would marry her. She was another woman who wasn't safe to be out in the world on her own.

Dubin told Paula and her father that he would like to speak to the Galotto family and to the Martelli brothers. It would be important for his thesis. Paula's father suddenly remembered that the following day, a Saturday, the town's five-a-side team would be playing, and the Martelli brothers, who financed the team, would be sure to be at the sports hall, especially since the match would mark the début of their newest signing, Mandioca. Given that Paula and her father were campaigning against Fabrizio, they couldn't really introduce Dubin to the Martelli brothers, but it wouldn't be hard for Dubin to approach them, for they really were very charming.

"Like all rogues," Afonso added.

I asked Dubin to enquire about the wife of Galotto the artist, and I read out to him what Ariadne had written about her mother, repeating the phrase that had struck me most: "The moon drags the sea after it like a dark crime."

"Bloody hell," Dubin said.

He promised to investigate further. Then he announced that he needed to go to bed. Paula had promised to give him a tour of the town and the surrounding area the following morning. And in the afternoon, he would go to the football match and try and speak to the Martelli brothers.

"Be careful. Don't forget that one or both of them might be murderers."

"We'll be in a sports hall full of people. I won't be in any danger."

"But be careful what you say. And phone me tomorrow night."

"Wouldn't you rather I give you a full report when I come back to Porto Alegre on Monday?"

"No. Ring me tomorrow."

Any head of operations needs to follow a mission closely. The

63

inside man depends on having an alert controller. And besides, Marcito was paying for the phone calls.

But Dubin did not phone the following night. I had stayed at home beneath the bewildered gaze of Julinha, João and Black the dog, waiting for the call and drinking nothing. He didn't phone on the Sunday either. Nor did he turn up at the office on Monday. I rang his home number. A woman I assumed to be his mother told me that Joel hadn't slept at home for the last three nights and, no, she had no idea where he was. I asked beautiful Bela if we had some way of contacting Túlio, who might still be in Frondosa. No, Túlio never stayed longer than a day in each town. He would have moved on to the next town by now, but she didn't know where. We tried to get the number of the hotel in Frondosa where Dubin had been staying. With no success. I started imagining what might have happened, to imagine the worst. Dubin meeting Franco Martelli in the sports hall during the football match. I imagined him forgetting himself for a moment and mentioning Ariadne, and Martelli immediately feeling suspicious. What do you know about my wife? What are you after? Diminutive Dubin, caught off guard, stammering some excuse or other that had only increased the betrayed husband's suspicions. Perhaps Dubin was, at that very moment, locked in some dungeon in Frondosa. Or perhaps, like the Secret Lover, he had already been eliminated. The Martelli brothers were bandits, capable of anything, of that I had no doubt. I left work early and dropped in at the school where Dubin taught.

No, he hadn't come to work, and they had heard nothing from him. I headed for the Bar do Espanhol, which, like Black, gave me an odd look. Me in the bar on a Monday? I needed to get together with the organising committee of Operation Theseus, but the only member present was Professor Fortuna, who advised me to keep calm. We should hold on for at least another two days. If Dubin still gave no sign of life, then we would act. We would put another man inside to find out what had happened.

"But who?"

"Me," Professor Fortuna said.

I ordered a *cachaça*.

7

"TO SPY IS TO WAIT." THE WORDS ARE JOHN LE CARRÉ'S. YOU put your agents in place and then wait to see what happens, wait for the reaction of those being spied upon, wait for their agent to show himself and hope that the worst doesn't happen. By the Wednesday, we'd still heard nothing from Dubin. He could have phoned me at home or at the office, but he didn't. His mother had no news of him either, although she didn't seem overly concerned. I assumed that it was not uncommon for Dubin to spend several nights away from home without calling to say where he was. I left the office at the end of the day and went to the Bar do Espanhol. I looked around, but Professor Fortuna was nowhere to be seen. I saw Tavinho sitting at a table with a clean-shaven man with slicked-back hair and wearing a blue blazer with gold buttons.

Only when I reached the table did I realise that the man was the Professor – utterly transformed. I had never seen him without his thick beard and his overcoat the colour of a wet rat. He pointed to the suitcase beside his chair and said, "In an hour's time I'm catching the night bus to Frondosa."

"Are you sure, Professor?" I felt a duty to protect him. I knew little about his life outside the Bar do Espanhol. I knew he was a poseur, but that was all. Perhaps he had no life outside the bar. Perhaps this was his first incursion into the real world. And I was responsible.

"I'm ready," he said.

"Wait a moment. We have to sort a few things out. I need to give you money for—"

"I have money. I've already bought my ticket."

Was the Professor an eccentric millionaire? I knew absolutely nothing about him.

"And what about your legend?" asked Tavinho, who loved jargon. "What are you going there as?"

"As a philosopher, a wandering philosopher in search of the truth."

"And why would you find the truth in Frondosa?"

He ignored my question and said, "If Dubin phones, tell him to come back, tell him the serious work is about to begin. This is a job for grown-ups." He was already getting to his feet when I thought to ask:

"If anything should happen to you, who should I contact?"

"What could possibly happen to me?" And he added, when he was already halfway out of the door, "Isn't this all just a fiction?"

To spy is to wait. At home, waiting for some sign from Dubin, I sat imagining the Professor on his night bus, travelling towards Frondosa, following the thread of our reverse Ariadne into the Labyrinth. I should have put a stop to this madness. The Professor was a complete mystery. If he disappeared as well, like Dubin, I wouldn't know what to do. I didn't know if he had family or if there was someone responsible for him. I knew nothing about his past, nothing at all. What had Ariadne and Frondosa awoken inside that dark mind, what dormant fantasies and hopes had they stirred into life? Then again, I could hardly feel surprised by this new, clean-shaven Professor with his gold buttons. Under Ariadne's spell, I too had changed. Not even my dog recognised me now. Besides, I thought, surely enigmas and poseurs made the best spies. The Professor had a penchant for pretence, perhaps he simply hadn't practised it in real life, outside the realms of literature and the Bar do Espanhol. The question was, how would real life receive this new, transformed Professor? In Frondosa, he...

The phone rang. It was Dubin. Talking about Paradise.

"I'm in heaven! I'm in heaven!"

"What's happened?"

"I'm in love!"

"Aren't you coming back?"

"That depends."

And Dubin told me that on Saturday morning, Paula had taken him for a drive around the town and the surrounding area. Near the house in the countryside where her father cultivated his roses, she had stopped by a babbling brook and they had made love among the insects and ticks in the shade of a fig tree. "Yes," he said, "brooks really do babble – just like they do in books. I heard it." And making love in the open air, on the grass, in the middle of the morning, was different from anything he had ever experienced before: "The smell of the earth! The smell of the cow dung! I had a positively telluric hard-on! Telluric!"

As they drove back into town, Paula had asked him what star sign he was and revealed that, according to *Astrology and Love*, their signs were not only compatible but complementary. They had what the book called "alpha compatibility, vertical and horizontal", which, according to Fulvio Edmar, was responsible for all the great love affairs in history. Still uncertain quite what to expect from Paula, Dubin recited his poem about the erect hypotenuse in search of a welcoming triangle, and the look of utter incomprehension on her face convinced him: he was definitely in love. That afternoon, they went to watch the five-a-side football match at the town's sports hall, to try and make contact with the Martelli brothers. And then Dubin announced, "I saw her."

"Sawer?"

"I – saw – her. Ariadne."

"What?!"

Ariadne sitting in the terraces. Arm-in-arm with her husband, Franco. Beside them, Fabrizio and his wife. Was Ariadne pretty? "Lovely." Did she seem sad? "No, just slightly distracted. She barely watched the game." How was she dressed? "Quite sportily. With her hair caught back. And, as far as I could see, she wasn't wearing any make-up."

"Did you manage to get close?"

"No, I couldn't. At the end of the match, I tried to go over to them, but I could see that Fabrizio was in a bad mood. His team had lost, despite a brilliant performance by the new player, Mandioca. They left the sports hall immediately."

"And she was arm-in-arm with her husband?"

"The whole time. If he did kill her lover, she's obviously forgiven him."

"What are the brothers like?"

"Franco is a good-looking chap with nice, thick hair. Fabrizio is older and fatter. Franco is more athletic-looking. Both are fairly dark-skinned and taller rather than shorter."

"Bastards."

I asked Dubin if Ariadne looked as if she had been sedated. Perhaps Franco had forced her to go out with him, to be seen arm-in-arm with him, to give the lie to any gossip.

"She did seem slightly out of it."

That was it. She had been sedated. Franco was a monster. At

home, he kept her locked in her room, where, underneath the covers, she wrote her denunciation of him, her cry for help, her suicide note. How much time did we have? She wouldn't kill herself before she finished the book, which, through the "friend", or, miraculously, on her own initiative, she was sending to the publisher in dribs and drabs. She wouldn't kill herself until she closed her heart. *Would* she kill herself? Or would her editor arrive in time to save her?

Dubin had still not met the Galotto brother who drank and played snooker in the bar next to the hotel. But that same Saturday night, Paula had taken him to the Arpege nightclub, where the well-to-do youth of the town went to dance, and where – with some difficulty, because the music was so loud they had to shout at each other – he had spoken to Lúcio Flávio, the tall, pale antiquarian who was the society columnist on the *Frondosa Folio* and who knew everything about everyone in the town. Lúcio had spent the night sucking some substance or other through a straw from various pineapples, and then had suddenly leapt to his feet, torn off his shirt, cried, "Clear the floor!" and started dancing, whirling his shirt above his head like a helicopter blade. Prior to lift-off, though, he had given Dubin the lowdown on the Galottos and the Martellis. He described Ariadne's father as an innocent and the Martelli brothers as very sharp businessmen. Gangsters? No, he wouldn't go that far. They had certainly put one over on the old man, but that's what businessmen do to artists. He himself was both businessman and artist, so knew both sides and had no illusions about human behaviour. Trying to be as casual as possible, Dubin asked what Lúcio Flávio knew about Ariadne. Very well read, Lúcio Flávio said. Well bred? No, well read. Well, both really. And very spoilt. She hadn't been brought up to marry into a family like the Martellis, with no name and no culture. It was said that Ariadne – who spoke four languages and could tell a Manet from a Monet – had agreed to marry Franco Martelli – for whom the only painter worth his salt was Cappelletti, so good they named a soup after him – in exchange for a loan that would help her father save the factory. However, as soon as they had Ariadne, the Martelli brothers had called in the loan and assumed control of the company. Then, very cautiously, Dubin asked if there were any rumours about Ariadne. Something about a lover...? No, Lúcio Flávio knew nothing about that. He just repeated what Paula had said, that Martelli was overly protective of Ariadne. She was hardly ever seen in town. She visited Lúcio's antiques shop now and then, but rarely bought anything. She said that she only went there "in order to visit the past". She went to ten o'clock Mass on Sundays in the church on the square, where she made her confession and took Communion. Occasionally, she would attend some social event with Franco, but spent most of her time shut up at home. By then, Lúcio Flávio was on his fifth or sixth pineapple and starting to bemoan his lot. He was a shitty little society columnist on a shitty little newspaper in a shitty little town. He could understand Ariadne, who came to his shop seeking refuge in the past from the cultural aridity of Frondosa. However, Lúcio Flávio felt sure that his talent would one day be recognised and that he would have his moment of glory. Yes, glory! And with that, he had leapt up from his zebra-skin pouffe and bounded onto the dance floor. (According to Dubin, Santa Edwige dos Aflitos has a nightclub just like Arpege, called Bora Bora, but without the zebra-skin pouffes.)

Dubin asked me not to tell his mother that he had been to Sunday Mass at the church on the square. His mother was always trying to persuade him to go to synagogue and would find it completely unacceptable that, not only had he visited a Catholic church, he had also knelt down in the aisle in front of the altar and made the sign of the cross. It was all part of his disguise. Ariadne was sitting in the front pew beside a strangely dark-skinned lady who looked as if she had just emerged from a coal mine. "That's the Martellis' mother," Paula explained, having entered the church arm-in-arm with Dubin. Senhora Martelli was not, in fact, dirty, she simply had a problem with blocked pores, hence her funereal appearance. She dozed off a couple of times during Father Bruno's sermon, even though he, being deaf, tended to shout. Dubin stored away the fact that she had dozed off. It might be of use later on. Ariadne stared fixedly at the altar, without once looking around. She stood up to receive the Host and went back to her seat without raising her eyes from the floor. She was wearing a black veil over her blonde hair. Dubin hadn't been able to find a seat near her and didn't know quite what he would have done if he had. He could hardly strike up a conversation in the middle of Mass or try to whisper in her ear. And whisper what? Outside the church, he asked Paula to introduce him to Ariadne.

"Why? I haven't spoken to her in years."

"I think it could be important for me to meet her, for my research, I mean . . ."

Ariadne had smiled broadly when she saw Paula. Dubin awarded her maximum points for her smile. Ten out of ten!

"Paulinha! It's been so long!"

"I know! This is Joel, a friend from Porto Alegre. He's a poet."

"A minor poet," Dubin said, shaking Ariadne's hand.

Another dazzling smile. Handshake: firm. Hand: slightly cold. But she hadn't looked him in the eye.

"We must see more of each other," Ariadne said to Paula.

"We live in the same town and yet we hardly see each other at all."

Yes, we really must make a firm date, etc., etc. Mwa, mwa. And Ariadne had said goodbye to Dubin, saying that she loved poetry and would like to read one of his poems some time.

"Best not, you might lose your taste for poetry altogether," Dubin said, and was rewarded with another perfect smile.

I asked him if he had, in any way, felt that he was in the presence of a potential suicide. Dubin said that the only thing that made him think of death during their meeting was the presence of the Martellis' swarthy mother, who had stood apart from them while they were talking, but was clearly listening to every word, like a hyper-alert security guard.

That afternoon, Paula and Dubin had returned to the rose garden, where, spiritually reinvigorated by their morning visit to the church and a roast-lamb lunch, they again made love beside the babbling brook. During what Dubin described as a post-coital pause, a time when people tend to indulge in highly personal confessions and reflections, they had told each other their respective life stories, Dubin's, of course, heavily embellished. Paula had already had one unhappy relationship: a husband who had channelled all his bitterness about life into comments about the size of her bum and who, in the end, had left her. Paula had sworn that she would never marry again. Dubin couldn't be entirely sure, but he thought, as he lay half-asleep in the shade of that ancient fig tree, incapable of distinguishing the hoarse song of the cicadas from the hum of satisfaction in his brain, that he had heard Paula whisper in his ear that she was ready to break that oath.

"Anyway," he added, "I'm now washing my underpants in the sink in my hotel room."

That Wednesday, Lúcio Flávio reported in his column in the *Frondosa Folio* that the town had received an important visitor – Joel Dubin, teacher, poet and sociologist – who was in Frondosa to carry out a study of the Galotto company. He went on to suggest that Fabrizio Martelli pay more attention to his business affairs

and abandon his attempt to be re-elected as mayor and his continued efforts to uglify the town, a decision that would win him the
wholehearted support of a grateful community. That same afternoon, Dubin had received a phone call at the hotel, saying that the
mayor would like to meet him. A visit to the town hall had been
arranged for the following day.

"So you're going to stay in Frondosa, are you?" I asked.

"Yes, at least for a few more days – or for the rest of my life if I
marry Paula."

"Don't you need any money?"

"I'm being sponsored by the Uruguayan! He's agreed to pay
Paula's father to take me on at the newspaper. And he's paying my
hotel bill too. I'm in heaven, my friend, in heaven! I just need to
buy a few clothes. Well, underpants at any rate. I'd better talk to
the Uruguayan about that."

"What's your role on the newspaper going to be?"

"Either cleaner or editor-in-chief, I'm not sure yet."

"And what about your classes? And your work here at the
publishing house?"

"Please, this is hardly the moment to remind me of my real
life."

"Call me at the office tomorrow."

"I will."

"And another thing . . ."

"What's that?"

"The Professor is coming to Frondosa. He should be there

77

tomorrow morning."

"Professor Fortuna?! Why's he coming here?"

"I haven't a clue. It was his idea. And you may not recognise him."

"Why?"

"He's shaved off his beard and is wearing a blazer with gold buttons."

"Bloody hell!"

8

MARCITO'S ARRIVAL AT THE OFFICE IS ALWAYS SOMETHING OF a spectacle. We hear the roar of his motorbike, hear him revving noisily as he manoeuvres into the parking space reserved for him on the pavement, and, finally, before he turns off the ignition, there are a last few explosions from the engine, like the stertorous groans of some dying monster. Then Marcito bursts through the door, still wearing his brightly coloured helmet. Every day, we are invaded by this same gigantic space insect.

On that particular Thursday, he asked, "So what's happened to Dubin?"

"He hasn't come back yet." I was about to add, "And he might never come back," but decided against it. That would have meant telling Marcito about the latest developments in Operation Theseus, and, besides, Marcito wasn't listening anymore. He had gone into his office, from where he called:

"Bela, will you come in, please?"

The beautiful Bela went into the office, shutting the door behind her. I turned my attention to the day's rather scant correspondence, which included an invitation to the launch in a few days' time of Corina's *Poems and Thoughts*, including drinks and a signing session. Written on the edge of the invitation were these words: "Hope to see you there, creep." There was also a white envelope from Frondosa. With the fourth chapter.

The previous night, I had dreamed of Ariadne. Or, rather, I had dreamed of an adolescent girl coming down a grand staircase, wearing a white dress and with her long, blonde hair falling onto her bare shoulders. The face wasn't the same as in the photograph. Her features were blurred, as if someone had tried to erase them. I was waiting for her at the bottom of the stairs, but she never reached me, and her features never became clear. It was as if the staircase were getting longer and longer as she descended and as if her face were growing more and more remote. I woke with a thought. In fact, it was the thought that woke me from the dream. If the Secret Lover could remember Ariadne coming down the stairs when she was fifteen, and remember her coming down the stairs when she was still a child, and, again as a child, getting frustrated over her piano practice, they must have been brought up together. The house of the catalpa tree belonged to both their memories, they had shared a past in that same house. Perhaps he was a cousin, or a childhood friend, or some other person who she had never imagined would become a lover. Becoming lovers was a profanation of their past, a re-appropriation, so that they could live it again in different bodies and with a different ending.

The fourth chapter was about the Secret Lover, whom she described, for some strange reason, as "a golden child the world will kill and eat". They had started meeting in the abandoned house, always at night. They made love on the floor, surrounded by the lit candles. Or they would climb what remained of the staircase to her old, now ceiling-less bedroom. Through the gaps in the roof, she could see the sky, which she described as carbon paper with holes in it, holes that let in "a bonewhite light like death behind all things". They made love with a kind of desperate fury. She was about to marry Franco, whom she identified in the text simply as "He". A date for the wedding had been set. Ariadne told the Secret Lover that they could not continue to meet after the wedding, and the Secret Lover begged her at least to go on meeting until the house of the catalpa tree was demolished, until there was nothing left of that ruined past to which they had returned and which they were now reliving, this time as lovers. She said that would be utter madness, and she wasn't mad. "I am," he said. "I always was." "No," she said, "you were always a child. You took the fact that we all grew up and you did not as a kind of betrayal." And he, his head between her breasts, said: "So did you return to the past to find me? Doesn't that constitute a rescue?" "No, you're the one who dragged me back to this innocent past in order to experience this new childhood. That's kidnapping."

One day, the Secret Lover showed her something: "Look what I've been writing." It was a diary of all their meetings at the ruined house, from the very first night. Everything they had done, everything they had said. She asked him to destroy the diary, but he refused. It would be what remained once the house had been destroyed, a memento of those days. "Anyway," he said, "who's to say the diary isn't pure fiction?" And she: "But it has my name in it – it's dangerous." And he: "The world is full of Ariadnes."

The golden child had turned up at the wedding dressed entirely in black. Black suit, black shirt, black tie and a ring in his nose. A month after her honeymoon in Punta del Este, Ariadne had passed the house of the catalpa tree, and there he was at the window, as if he were waiting for her, as if they had arranged a time to meet. He didn't wave, he merely smiled. She went up the cracked steps to the front door, which stood open, as if it, too, were expecting her, and she entered, uttering a cry somewhere between a moan, a sob and a shriek of joy, she couldn't tell, but whatever it was, it signified a surrender to madness. "I read somewhere that the Greek word for 'seduce' also means 'destroy'. I don't know if I seduced him by bringing him back from his perenial childhood –" she wrote "perennial" with one "n" – "or if he seduced me back into the past whether it was a rescue or a kidnapping," Ariadne wrote,

82

as economical with commas as ever, "but the fact is that we destroyed each other. Soon I will take my own life as did Ariadne abandoned on the island of Naxos while he has already been murdered and devoured by concrete."

The word *concrete* made me jump. "Concrete"?! Had Franco killed the Secret Lover – or ordered him to be killed – and had him buried in concrete? Gangsters! They were gangsters. Franco kept Ariadne sedated and under constant watch. She could only leave the house accompanied by the funereal mother-in-law Dubin had described. She went to Sunday Mass and to five-a-side football matches, clinging submissively to her husband's arm. And she spent the rest of the time shut up in the house, guarded by gangsters, writing her long-suicide-note-in-chapters. Or perhaps it wasn't a suicide note, but a cry for help. The Ariadne myth has two endings, depending on which version you read. In one version, abandoned by Theseus on the island of Naxos, she kills herself. In the other, she is saved by Dionysus, who becomes her lover and with whom she achieves eternal happiness, the happiness of the gods. Ariadne's text was a plea to Dionysus, any Dionysus, even a middle-aged one with incipient cirrhosis of the liver, to save her from her past and change her future. I needed to go to Frondosa, as a god and as an editor. But not yet, not yet.

Later that afternoon, Dubin phoned. He sounded sleepy. The shameless creature was probably lying in bed with Paula beside him. But he was full of news. First of all, he didn't know what had become of Professor Fortuna. He knew that the Professor had checked into the hotel early that morning, but he hadn't seen him anywhere. The Professor was on the loose in Frondosa, doing quite what, he couldn't imagine. Dubin, meanwhile, had been to the town hall, where he had been received warmly by Fabrizio, who had asked him about his research. Dubin had explained that he was carrying out a study on the way family businesses changed hands in Rio Grande do Sul and how the Galotto case seemed to him fairly typical. Fabrizio offered to arrange a visit to the factory and to set up a meeting with his brother Franco, who was the one in charge of running the business. Both men stood up, and after Dubin had thanked Fabrizio for his help and they had shaken hands, the mayor abandoned the formal tone in which he had been speaking up until then and launched into a rather surprising conversation, with one hand resting on Dubin's shoulder. (Dubin's diminutive stature seems to inspire feelings of instant intimacy in people.)

"You've probably heard bad things about me," Fabrizio said, smiling. "The mayor who chops down trees and replaces them with concrete."

Dubin didn't know what to say. He stammered:

"N-no. I mean . . ."

"They're quite right. I ordered the tree in the middle of the square to be cut down, the tree that gave the town its name. Very sad. It was a wonderful tree. But what they don't mention is that the tree was dead. There was a risk that a branch could fall on someone's head, on a child's head . . ."

"Of course."

"The tree could have fallen on the head of Galotto, one of the factory's former owners, who used to get drunk every night and pee at its foot. It occurred to me that it was Galotto's urine that had killed the tree. And then what would people have said about the mayor?"

"Quite."

"In a way, the same thing happened with the factory. It was bankrupt, rotten. The Galotto family were highly respected, part of the town's history, but they had no idea how to run a business. The old man was an artist, he lived to travel, spending money he didn't have. And his children . . ." Fabrizio left the sentence hanging. The children, he was implying, were rotten as well. "We saved the factory. We saved thousands of jobs," he went on. "But they don't mention that either."

Dubin guessed that the mayor already knew about his relationship with Paula and was sending a message through him to her father.

Dubin's other piece of news? He had finally met Ariadne's older brother, Ariosto Galotto, in the bar next door to the hotel. Impeccably dressed, complete with tie and waistcoat. It was mid-afternoon, and Ariosto was already drunk, but the brandy had not yet fuddled his tongue or affected his snooker style. This was the first and last time that Dubin managed to have a normal conversation with him. Dubin had asked after his sister, and Ariosto had replied that he had lunch with her every Thursday, "poor thing".

Why "poor thing"?

"Because I'm the only person who visits her, apart from members of her husband's family. She spends all her time in that great mansion, hardly ever going out. She has no friends . . ."

Dubin told Galotto what the mayor had said about him, and Galotto burst out laughing.

"It's true, and I still pee in the square every night. My aim is to destroy that hideous concrete circle with my pee."

Ariosto Galotto wasn't the only picturesque character Dubin had met that evening. Frondosa had far surpassed Santa Edwige dos Aflitos as regards eccentrics. Paula had introduced him to Rico, a pale young man with dark circles under his eyes and an ugly indentation in one temple, and whose thin, cold hand Dubin shook as tentatively as if it were the hand of a corpse. Later, Paula told him Rico's story. Rico wasn't his real name. He had made a suicide pact with his girlfriend because her parents refused to accept their relationship. She had stolen her father's pistol so that they could kill themselves. She would shoot him and then shoot herself in the head. Miraculously, though, the bullet did not penetrate her boyfriend's skull. He merely fainted. Horrified at what she had done or perhaps frightened by the sheer volume of the blast, the girl had flung down the gun and run away. Rico soon recovered consciousness, and his explanation as to why the bullet had not killed him had remained the same to that day: "It ricocheted."

From then on, he was known as the Ricochet Kid, which, over time, became shortened to "Rico". The girlfriend's parents, shocked by the near-tragedy brought about by their intolerance, had changed their minds completely and allowed the couple to continue seeing each other. The girl, however, no longer wanted Rico, partly – or so it was said – because the dent in his temple had left him disfigured. Rico went on to get a degree in accounting, which was surprising really, since before he was shot, he had been completely useless at maths. And he started writing poetry. He was even president of the Poets' Club (another enterprise financed by the Uruguayan), which met once a week in a backroom of Fotos Mazaretto, which doubled as a bookshop and photo-copying centre. Rico had a curious habit: he didn't mind people being able to see the dent in his forehead, but when he visited Loló's brothel, he wore a mask covering his whole face. "Out of respect," he said. And whereas all the other men who frequented Loló's house made a point of disguising the fact that they were going to a brothel, when Rico went, he would don his mask and walk across town and past his former girlfriend's house, so that everyone would know precisely where he was going and know, too, that while the ricocheting bullet may have transformed him into a mathematician and a poet, it had not affected his sexual powers.

*

The Uruguayan's guilt-fuelled generosity knew no limits. As well as paying for the hire of the room where Rico and the town's other poets met to read their work and hold literary evenings, he supported Paula's father's newspaper, bought Mandioca for the Martellis' five-a-side team – despite his newspaper's opposition to the mayor – and ensured that Loló's brothel continued to operate in its traditional location behind the cemetery. Dubin told me all this in almost ecstatic tones. To get to Loló's brothel, you had to take a short cut through the cemetery. According to him, the expression "I'm going to visit Mama's grave", so often given to explain visits to the cemetery that were really a cover for visits to Loló's, had become part of the town's folklore, and lost all credibility when it began to be used even by husbands whose mothers were still alive and kicking. Another curious figure was Paula's father, Afonso, who had travelled the world and, so his daughter told Dubin, had even spent a longish period in the Soviet Union, returning to his native town in order to set up the *Frondosa Folio*, in which he wrote occasional articles about ancient problems in Communist Party doctrine, articles that few read and no-one understood. He said that his old compulsion to change the world now found its outlet in the revolutionary experiments he was carrying out on roses in pursuit of what he called "the perfect red". He left the newspaper's more modern causes, like holding to account the town's highly un-ecological mayor, to Paula and her young friends. Dubin had managed to win Afonso's heart by claiming to nurse a secret admiration for Stalin.

*

This was all very picturesque, but he should be focused on pursuing the aims of Operation Theseus. The first thing on Dubin's mind should be locating Professor Fortuna before he did something foolish that might compromise the mission, our main objective being to reach Ariadne without arousing the suspicions of the bastards keeping her under guard. Then he should investigate the possibility (which seemed obvious to me) that Ariosto Galotto was the person sending us his sister's manuscripts. He had lunch with her every week and would have found it easy enough to smuggle out the sheets of paper, photocopy them and mail them off to the publishing house. That would explain the shaky writing on the envelope – not a child's writing, but a drunk's. And he, who might or might not be an accomplice in Ariadne's revenge on her husband and in her denunciation-cum-last will and testament, must be the person who picked up my letters from the P.O. Box. The "friend" did not exist – it was Ariadne herself. And another thing: "See if you can find out what happened to the younger brother, and how that concrete circle in the middle of the square was made?"

"Are those two things connected in some way?"

I told Dubin what Ariadne had written about the Secret Lover. It was possible that the "golden child" was her younger brother and that his body had been swallowed up by the concrete in the square. Dubin's response was concise: "Bloody hell."

"Doesn't Paula remember seeing the younger brother dressed

entirely in black at the wedding?"

"No. All she said was that he was handsome and had the same dreamy, romantic look as me. Although without my charm, of course."

"Be careful, Dubin. Frondosa is a dangerous place for poets, even minor ones."

"I'm a real hit here. Paula won't let me out of her sight, her father addresses me as 'comrade', and I think the mayor would like to adopt me . . ."

"Be careful, Dubin."

It was late by the time I left the office. I had been reading and re-reading what Ariadne had written about the Secret Lover. At home, I ordered a pizza over the phone. Have I mentioned that Julinha had given up on me, taken João with her and gone to live with her sister? She couldn't stand me when I was drunk, then discovered that I was even more unbearable sober. I was left alone with Black the dog. But he's not speaking to me either.

9

AT THE BAR, MIGUEL DE UNAMUNO RECEIVED ME WITH A GLUM face. My abstinence was losing him money. That Friday night, as I reported back to Tavinho and Fulvio Edmar on what was happening in Frondosa, on Joel Dubin's adventures in a place he might have invented himself, I drank only a glass of mineral water. I hesitated before telling Fulvio Edmar that *Astrology and Love* was widely read in Frondosa, and that his book had been a major factor in Ariadne's decision to send us her story. All the more reason to demand the royalties that Marcito was refusing to pay him "so as not to set a dangerous precedent". Marcito dislikes authors in general, especially those who demand what is rightfully theirs. He finds the idea of someone wanting to be paid as well as published a particularly repulsive, almost obscene form of literary pretention.

*

"Any news of the Professor?" Tavinho asked.

"None. He arrived, checked into the hotel and vanished."

I asked if Tavinho knew of a five-a-side player called Mandioca.

"Yes. He's a fantastic player, but a bit . . ." Tavinho paused for a moment to choose the right word: "Problematic."

"What do you mean?"

"He's something of a gypsy. He never stays long on any team. He likes to party. And they say he takes backhanders to fix matches. But he's a fantastic player. Why?"

"He's playing for Frondosa."

"They'd better watch out then . . ."

The latest news from Frondosa was that our man inside had met Franco Martelli. He had been shown round the factory by him and invited to lunch at his house. Into the monster's lair! The house was in a residential area away from the town centre. An enormous, hyper-modern place. The swimming pool was in the shape of a comma, which Dubin considered in some way significant. No, Ariadne hadn't joined them for lunch. Franco, like everyone else, quickly warmed to little Dubin. He spoke openly about taking over the Galotto factory. He described old Galotto as "an extraordinary figure", an artist who had not the faintest idea about running a business. And without Dubin even mentioning Ariadne's name, he volunteered: "She's a very fragile person." He could have been describing a piece of rare porcelain, thus justifying the special care she required and, in a way, justifying her absence from the lunch table. Then he added:

"I believe you two have already met . . ."

The monster knew about Dubin and Ariadne's brief encounter outside the church. Nothing escaped him. Not a single tiny chip on the porcelain.

Dubin ventured to ask:

"Could I possibly interview her about her father, about the factory?"

Franco had smiled and said simply, "No."

The Martellis' five-a-side team would be playing again on Saturday. Dubin would go to the game and try to strike up a conversation with Franco and Ariadne. Paula had resisted his suggestion that she try to arrange a meeting with Ariadne, perhaps a visit to her house, a tea party for old friends in the afternoon, when – although Dubin didn't say this – Franco would not be there. Paula had refused. She didn't like Dubin's insistence on meeting Ariadne, however often he assured her that such a meeting was necessary for his research and that his interest was purely sociological. No, she didn't like it at all. Dubin would try to speak to Ariadne at the sports hall, perhaps slip her a note. But saying what? He didn't know. And what if one of the brothers saw him passing her the note? It was dangerous. He, too, might end up being swallowed by concrete.

*

Dubin reported that he had decided to speak frankly to Ariosto Galotto and ask if he was the person who took his sister's manuscripts to be photocopied at Fotos Mazaretto and then mailed them to the publisher. Did he read what Ariadne wrote, did he know of her intention to commit suicide once she'd had her revenge on her husband by publishing the book? And did he know what had happened to his younger brother? Dubin, however, only managed to talk to Galotto late that night, when the drunk's brain was already addled by alcohol. He had to follow him out to the square, where Galotto peed on the great concrete circle just as he did every night. Galotto had walked stiffly but steadily across the road, his tie and waistcoat still impeccable, but his answers to Dubin's questions resembled incoherent oratory: "One generation dies, another takes its place. The last will be the . . . Then it stops. Everything stops. Do you see? It just stops. That's all."

"Do you know about the book Ariadne is writing?"

"Ve-ry gra-du-al-ly. Gra-du . . . What's that? Oh, it's my cock." In the middle of peeing, Galotto smiled. He had thought of a phrase: "The last will *beat* the first. Eh? Eh?"

Dubin tried again: "Do you know what happened to your brother?"

"I am the lasht . . . I am the lasht . . . No, I am the rain . . ."

And with that, Galotto tilted his cock to try and reach the centre of the concrete circle with his pee.

*

On Sunday, Dubin phoned to tell me what had happened on Saturday. Still no news of the Professor, who had quite simply vanished. The staff at the hotel reception knew nothing about him. He hadn't slept in his room, though his suitcase was still there. Most mysterious. The five-a-side match had been amazing. The Galotto team had won, thanks to some spectacular play by Mandioca. The following Saturday's match would be decisive, and almost all of Frondosa would be accompanying the team to the next town to watch. In the sports hall, Dubin had managed to sit near the Martellis, despite Paula's protests. The brothers had given him a friendly wave; Ariadne had waved too and smiled vaguely. At half-time, Franco and Fabrizio had gone down to the dressing room, presumably to speak to the trainer, and Dubin had thought this would be his chance to speak to Ariadne, who had remained on the terrace with Fabrizio's wife. Dubin described the two women as "an oasis of blondeness". But he did not get very far. According to Dubin, "a large brown fridge" blocked his attempt to approach with a "Sorry, sir" and a large hand on his chest. Only then did Dubin realise that four rugby players were guarding the two women, one at each point of the compass. He had waved again at Ariadne from beneath the muscular arm holding him at bay and said, "I wanted to show you my poems," but she had merely nodded and smiled vaguely again, without looking him in the eye. Did she seem sedated? She did. Perhaps she hadn't even heard what he had said. Dubin could see no way of getting close to Ariadne. When not escorted by that gloomy mother-in-law, she was either with her husband or surrounded by that phalanx of wardrobes. The only way would be to get into the house and catch her on her own, but, unless he was very much mistaken, the fences he had noticed when he had gone to lunch with Franco were electrified. And it wouldn't surprise him to learn that murderous dogs roamed the gardens. He had to lure Ariadne out of her captivity, to a place where her guards would be unable to prevent him making contact, just once.

"Be careful, Dubin."

"I will."

"And try to find the Professor."

"I will."

"What's your job on the newspaper, then?"

"I'm assistant something or other, I'm not quite sure what. I spend most of my time talking to Afonso. He says we're the last two Stalinists alive."

"And Paula?"

"Oh, we're fine. Except that I came out in the most terrible rash after all that rolling around in the undergrowth. No more telluric hard-ons. It's back to civilisation for me. So we went to a motel, called, can you believe it, 'Topaz'. Like the Hitchcock film."

In Dubin's Santa Edwige dos Aflitos, the main hotel was called "The Dark Red Eiderdown".

"Did you buy some new underwear?"

"The Uruguayan bought me a complete trousseau. I'm ready to get married!"

*

Marcito had authorised a new edition of *Astrology and Love*. Now that Fulvio Edmar and I were on speaking terms, and now that I was a new man since reading Ariadne's book and stopping drinking, Fulvio felt able to ask me if the publisher would finally pay him what he was owed. I told him I would speak to Marcito, but that I couldn't promise anything. I really had changed. I reviewed the unsolicited manuscripts that arrived in the office with fatherly benevolence. I didn't reject a single one. I wrote back saying that our editorial board would read their work and urging them not to feel discouraged if they didn't hear from us at once, because, whatever the verdict, it would not imply a judgement on their talent. The main thing was not to let any possible rejection clip the wings of a literary vocation that might just need a little more time in order to take flight. My letters were not just an incentive to new writers, they were an exaltation of literature itself and of that magnificent compulsion that leads people to want to produce something out of nothing. And if, for some reason, our editorial board were to advise against publishing their work, the author could always opt to pay to have the book published, for (and this was something the author might not realise) even the greatest writers in the world had occasionally done just that. I don't know if it was my abstinence from alcohol or Ariadne's spell or the magic of those comma-less texts that touched me with their sensitivity, their despair and their surprising turns of phrase, but the fact is that I had mellowed. I remembered the nights I used to spend reading obsessively, like a religious devotee, hunched beneath the bedclothes with the bedside lamp when my mother ordered me to stop reading and go to sleep; I recalled my own fantasies about becoming a writer and joining the fraternity of those who created such literary marvels. Dubin used to say that bad literature was literature in its purest state, untouched by the distractions of style, invention, wit or meaning, reduced to the simple impetus to write, to that magnificent compulsion. He said this to provoke me during our interminable arguments in the Bar do Espanhol, but under the spell of Ariadne's work, and with my native misanthrophy dissolved by mineral water, I had to admit that he was right. Those of us who feel the urge to write – even Corina – deserve to belong to the writing brotherhood of writers. It was an admirable impulse, regardless of whether one had any talent or not, even if it sprang from the need to open a wounded heart before it closed for ever, as was the case with my tragic Ariadne, or to produce nonsense like . . . like . . . Like Fulvio Edmar's *Astrology and Love*. Taking advantage of my new-found tolerance for the human race, Fulvio made a proposal: if the publisher sold him the whole of the latest print-run of *Astrology and Love* at cost price, he would set about selling the copies himself and keep any profit. Starting with Frondosa, where, it seemed, he had a large public. I said I would speak to Marcito.

Some important news from Frondosa: Dubin had finally located Professor Fortuna. He found him sitting in a bar having a beer with Rico, he of the dented forehead. The Professor had pretended not to know Dubin, who, understanding his caution, went over to the table to say hello to Rico, but gave no indication that he and the Professor already knew each other. They were, after all, both engaged on a secret mission. Later, in the Arpege nightclub, Dubin learned from Lúcio Flávio – who knew everything that went on in the town – the reason behind that encounter between the Professor and Rico. The Professor had offered to give a lecture at the Poets' Club, of which Rico was president. The lecture would be about . . . here Dubin paused for dramatic effect before shouting, "De Chirico!"

"What?!"

"Professor Fortuna will be giving a lecture about the painter De Chirico to the Poets' Club in Frondosa."

"But what does he know about De Chirico?"

"Probably nothing. He'll invent it on the spot."

Dubin had more to tell. He had found out a little about Ariadne's mother, whom everyone described as a very drab woman who had pre-deceased her husband and who was apparently nothing like the description her daughter gave of her. As for the concrete circle in the middle of the square, it had been laid very quickly, as soon as the great tree had been cut down, in record time, in fact. A team from the town hall had worked through the night to clear the square and level the concrete. As for Ariadne's younger brother, no-one could remember when he had last been seen. His disappearance might or might not have coincided with the rapid installation of the concrete circle. Ariosto Galotto had been of no help at all. Dubin had once more failed to get any information from him about his younger brother, to whom Galotto referred as "an angel, an angel".

Dubin tried again: "What happened to him?"

"Who?"

"Your younger brother."

"An angel, an angel . . ."

Ariadne had called the Secret Lover "a golden child", but until she was able to tell us more about his fate, it was impossible to know if there was a body buried underneath the concrete circle. Or if the body was that of an angel.

Dubin agreed with me: Professor Fortuna had, perhaps accidentally, stumbled upon the right strategy. A lecture about De Chirico would be sure to attract Ariadne and lure her from her house. Her father had known the artist in Italy. She owed her name to the painter's obsession with Ariadne. She might know a lot about his life and work and be interested to learn more from Professor Fortuna. It was such an irresistible coincidence, having an expert on De Chirico turn up like that in Frondosa, her town, her father's hometown. Her husband would be unlikely to accompany her to the talk. The burly guards who had surrounded her at the sports hall wouldn't fit in the tiny backroom at Fotos Mazaretto. That only left the dark-complexioned mother-in-law. However, one could almost certainly depend on her falling asleep at some point, and that would be Dubin's chance to speak to Ariadne. Thanks to Professor Fortuna, Operation Theseus was close to achieving its goal. All of this depended, of course, on Ariadne taking the bait and turning up at the lecture.

Lúcio Flávio duly announced in his column in the *Frondosa Folio* that the well-known critic, philosopher and teacher Professor Fortuna would be speaking about the painter Giorgio de Chirico at the Poets' Club on Saturday. Admission would be free. That same day, a delegation would be accompanying the Galotto five-a-side team to the next town for the semi-finals of the regional championship. Franco would go with the team and wouldn't be back until late that night. Would Ariadne go with him or stay in Frondosa? Would the monster force her to accompany him or allow her to attend the lecture? We would only find out on Saturday, when the Professor, with his frowning face and his gold buttons, would reveal everything he knew about the painter De Chirico, or perhaps invent everything he didn't know.

The Professor and Dubin met secretly in the Professor's hotel room. The two spies could not risk being seen together. The Professor explained his disappearance. On the night bus from Porto Alegre, he had met a very sweet girl who had invited him to spend a couple of nights at her house in Frondosa or, rather, at the home of her Aunt Loló, whom she was visiting. The Professor had left his suitcase at the hotel, grabbed a toothbrush and some underwear, and followed the girl through the cemetery to her aunt's house. Aunt Loló lived with her four daughters, who received their boyfriends and gentleman friends in their rooms. The Professor described how he had initiated the girl from the bus into the mysteries of tantric sex, of which he had been a pioneer in Rio Grande do Sul, and brought her to orgasm several times a day. After three days, however, there was a dispute over money, which the ungrateful girl insisted on being given despite those multiple orgasms, while Aunt Loló threatened to call the police, so that, in the end, the Professor had found himself obliged to pay up and leave. In that house by the cemetery, he had also met the football player, Mandioca – who had gone there to celebrate his team's victory with three of Aunt Loló's daughters at once – as well as an intriguing masked man who was courting one of the girls, and with whom Fortuna had spoken at length about art, life and the feminine mystique. And the masked man had accepted the Professor's offer to give a lecture on De Chirico in the room hired by the Poets' Club.

Dubin and the Professor agreed on the format of the lecture, should Ariadne turn up. Dubin had noticed that her swarthy mother-in-law had a tendency to doze off. In the church, he had seen her head nod several times during deaf Father Bruno's very loud sermon. It therefore didn't matter what the Professor said or at what volume. He could spout any nonsense he wanted as long it was in a sufficiently boring monotone to send the mother-in-law to sleep and give Dubin a chance to speak to Ariadne.

The Professor was offended by that reference to him "spouting nonsense": "I know all there is to know about De Chirico."

They phoned me from the hotel room to receive their instructions. What should Dubin say to Ariadne if he got the chance?

"Tell her I'm on my way, that I need to talk to her. And remember, my name is Agomar Trapiche. No, not Trapiche, Peniche. Or is it Trapiche? Anyway, just say Agomar."

"Alright."

The Professor had only one doubt about his lecture: "Do you say 'De Kirico' or 'De Shirico'?"

They both plumped for "De Kirico". That was how Tavinho had pronounced it, and he knew everything.

10

WHEN DUBIN PHONED TO REPORT BACK ON HOW THE LECTURE had gone, his first question was: "Did De Chirico have a mechanical leg?"

"I don't know. Why?"

"I asked the Professor if it was true that De Chirico had had an affair with Ivona Gabor. He said it was, but that the affair was very short-lived because Ivona couldn't cope with his mechanical leg."

"Oh honestly, you—" I began, irritated by their lack of seriousness.

"Calm down," Dubin said, interrupting me, "everything went to plan. Ariadne came, and I sat next to her. The mother-in-law went to sleep as predicted, and I told Ariadne that you would be coming to Frondosa to talk to her about the book."

"What did she say?"

"Nothing. She just nodded. She seemed confused."

"You mean she didn't say anything all evening?"

"She did ask the Professor a few questions. She asked about the influence of De Chirico's paintings on the other arts, such as poetry. And she asked the Professor if he agreed with her that the Ariadne paintings were really about loneliness."

"And how did the Professor do?"

"Well, if he *was* inventing it all, he was pretty convincing. He even threw in a long quotation from Nietzsche – in German. That was what sent the mother-in-law to sleep."

"The Professor speaks German?!"

"Well, no-one was quite sure *what* it was. It sounded like German."

"So what did you arrange with Ariadne?"

"Nothing. I said that you could meet her wherever she wanted. And I gave her a card from the hotel with your name written on the back: Agomar."

"And what did she say?"

"She took the card, but didn't say anything. I told her again that I would like to show her my poems some time, and she just smiled. Then she declined Rico's invitation to join us at the Uruguayan's restaurant, thanked the Professor for his lecture and left."

"Was she very pretty?"

"Very. Pretty, but sad."

*

106

Frondosa's team had thrashed their rivals from the next town, thanks again to some brilliant play by Mandioca. His regular visits to Loló's house didn't seem to be affecting his performance. On the contrary. He had confided to Rico that he needed to have sex every day in order to stay in shape. Something to do with keeping his body fluids in balance. The next game would be decisive for the regional championship, and in the town they talked of nothing else. They had to keep an eye on Mandioca, though. Since he was a crucial player, and since he was known to accept bribes to fix matches and even, depending on the size of the bribe, score an own goal, a plan was hatched to keep him away from any outside influences and thus deliver him from temptation. He would only be allowed to leave the hotel for training sessions. There was a rumour that someone was due to arrive that week with a sack of money with which to bribe him. The Professor overheard Mandioca himself telling Loló's girls about the expensive presents he would buy them once the championship was over. Even the town's old distrust of the Uruguayan resurfaced: if he was seen placing bets against Frondosa, as he had against Brazil in 1950, he would be cross-examined and forced to tell everything he knew about any plans to fix the match. True, it had been the Uruguayan who had bought Mandioca in order to strengthen the team, but a traitor is always a traitor. A general warning was issued. Everyone should be on the lookout for strangers carrying large bags.

*

Dubin asked if it wasn't time to include some local agents in Operation Theseus. Paula and her father and Lúcio Flávio could be recruited, if they knew what our mission was. Ariosto Galotto would be a natural ally – and could possibly help in elucidating his brother's death, if my suspicion that he was buried under the square proved to be true. Unfortunately, he was only sober, or reasonably sober, for a brief period on Thursdays, when he went to have lunch with Ariadne, and Dubin had not yet managed to catch him at the right time. I, however, disagreed with the idea of revealing our mission. We had to proceed with caution. The slightest mistake and Ariadne's life could be in peril, not to mention the lives of those involved in Operation Theseus and their accomplices. We were, after all, dealing with gangsters. Ariadne had written that like the cat she had nine times to die. This time she would die leaving behind her a very serious accusation. It would, however, be her last death, her definitive death. And the merest slip could precipitate that death.

"So when are you coming to Frondosa?" Dubin asked.

"When the time is right, but not now, not now."

How could we reveal our mission to anyone else when I still didn't know what it was?

The Professor's lecture had attracted a very small audience, but the members of the Poets' Club had greatly enjoyed it and invited him to give a second lecture on another subject of his choosing. The Professor had chosen "Neoplatonism in Dostoevsky and

Machado de Assis". His ideas met with great success in the bar next door to the hotel, where he asked only that people did not crowd him too much. Dubin acted as provocateur: "Professor, what about your theory that syphilis lies behind everything that Shakespeare wrote?"

The Professor would rub his face with his hands and begin "Everyone knows that..."

Dubin met with equal success among Paula's young friends, and with her father, who attributed the rebirth of his revolutionary faith to his conversations with Dubin about Stalin. Dubin, meanwhile, was continuing his espionage work. He had discovered that on the site of the house where Ariadne had grown up there was now an eight-storey block of flats – built by the Martelli brothers, who also owned a construction company. The name of the block was...

"Guess what."

"Ariadne."

"Right."

The only thing was that no-one could remember there ever having been a catalpa tree growing in front of the old house.

Dubin planned to attempt to talk to Ariadne at church on Sunday, trusting that Father Bruno's sermon would lull her mother-in-law to sleep again. Perhaps Ariadne would suggest a place where she and I could meet. And then I would *have* to go to Frondosa.

"We'll see," I said. I still can't explain why the prospect of coming face to face with Ariadne filled me with feelings of both panic and warm anticipation, feelings that had their epicentre in my belly. I didn't know what I would do in Frondosa; I only knew that whatever it was would define my life. Or perhaps the sensation of heat in the pit of my stomach was common to all those who approach the entrance to a labyrinth. I bet there's a word in German for the fear of disappearing for ever.

The letter accompanying the manuscript that arrived that week, containing the fifth chapter, was signed by Ariadne. The fiction of the "friend" sending the manuscripts without the author's knowledge had been abandoned entirely. There was no doubt now: it was Ariadne herself who gave the manuscripts to her brother to copy and send. In her letter, she said that if, despite her pleas not to come, I did decide to go to Frondosa, it was important that no-one should know of my visit or of the possibility that the book would be published. No-one knew that the book was being written. "The book isn't ready yet and although I would prefer you not to come if you do then please be very very discrete. Ariadne." The lack of commas and the spelling of "discrete" told me that the letter was authentic. And the fifth chapter was about the death and burial of the Secret Lover.

"I am ready for enormity," Ariadne wrote. Another of her obscure expressions. I assumed that she meant that she was ready for the violent denouement of the drama she had lived through, ready for vengeance and suicide. Another sentence: "How I would like to believe in tenderness – the face of the effigy gentled by candles bending on me in particular its mild eyes." Who was she referring to? Perhaps to her mother. To the desire to see her mother set down as an effigy on the floor of the old house, watching her two children embracing among the lit candles. And forgiving them, loving them. Who better to understand incest than a stone effigy, an ancient witness to human weakness? An effigy was sure to be more understanding than a distant, malevolent moon. Was that it? But what was an effigy doing in the middle of the story?

No tenderness or forgiveness awaited the two lovers. The cruel ending was swift in coming. One day the husband had gone into the house he was about to have demolished and found the Secret Lover. "He didn't care that he was there," wrote Ariadne:

> He knew he was a spoilt child who had never worked in his life and who had always behaved strangely. After all hadn't he worn a ring in his nose and for some inexplicable reason attended her wedding dressed in deepest mourning? The Secret Lover was what he called "one of the poets" those people who live in another world and contribute nothing to society but who are inoffensive and sometimes even amusing. He used to call my father "one of the poets of the world" someone

who needed to be protected from his own innocence. He warned the Secret Lover that the demolition of the house was about to begin and that it would be best if he started clearing out his little den, taking with him his crumpled sheet the candles and the rest of his junk – like this notebook. He picked it up from the floor and started leafing through the diary of our meetings that the Secret Lover had entitled "The house of the catalpa tree – The return". The Secret Lover tried to snatch the diary from his hands but he pushed him away and continued reading and the expression on his face went through several slow stages – curiosity horror bewilderment and anger – as he realised what it was he was reading.

He had then left abruptly, taking the diary with him and ordering the Secret Lover not to leave the house. When Ariadne arrived later that evening, she was surprised that the candles had not been lit to welcome her. The Secret Lover was sitting on the floor, his arms hanging limply at his sides like broken wings, a fallen angel:

> He told me what had happened and I said "Run!" but he shook his head. He would stay and let what had to happen happen. "Nothing *has* to happen!" I yelled. "Leave Frondosa!" No. He wouldn't run away. He would stay and wait for what had to happen for what was

written in the stars. He would try to explain that the diary was merely the working out of an obsession that none of it was true. That he was "one of the poets" and that everything in the diary was pure imagination. But I knew it would make no difference and that they would kill him. I was the one who shouldn't be there when they came for him. I was the one who should flee. But I didn't.

When her husband arrived, accompanied by two men, to take the Secret Lover away, he didn't even look at Ariadne. He didn't say anything. The Secret Lover started to explain that the diary was a fiction, the work of a poet, but, in an almost affectionate gesture, the husband put a finger to his lips, counselling silence. Ariadne asked what they were going to do with the Secret Lover, but received no answer. They left her alone in the silence of the great empty room, surrounded by the burnt-out stumps of candles. She went home. Her husband was there.

We ate supper together in silence. Afterwards his brother came and said that everything had been arranged. The installation of the concrete circle would be brought forward and that night the body would be hidden for ever. They spoke as if I wasn't there. He knew I would come home. He knew I would listen to what they were going to do with my

lover's body and say nothing. He knew I would
accept his verdict – "You're ill" – which was the only
thing he said to me that night and that I would agree
to live in silence and under guard until death came
to purge my guilt. The only thing he didn't know
was that my last death would come quickly and that
I would leave this final testament. To purge us all.

She's told the whole story now, I thought. What else can there be
left to tell? The rest of the book could only consist of childhood
reminiscences. The house of the catalpa tree, part one. Or her life
as a recluse since the death of her lover, surrounded by security
guards and murderous dogs and under sedation most of the time,
but always spinning the thread of her revenge. Perhaps the book
only needed those five chapters. "The book isn't ready yet," she had
said in the letter, but what was missing? It would be up to me,
as editor, to suggest ways of filling it out if necessary, as well
as adding some commas. She could include her adolescent years
in Frondosa, the dances at the club, her life as a member of one
of those minor aristocracies in what Dubin referred to, with
affectionate metropolitan disdain, as "our insane provinces". The
trips to Europe, the wedding. All converging on that dramatic
finale, her affair with the Secret Lover and his end, the revelation
– or not, it would depend on her – that the lover, the angel, the
golden child, was her brother and, finally, the naming of his execu-
tioners. And then her suicide. Good grief, I had forgotten about

her suicide. The five chapters were short because they were a suicide note. Dying *is* an art like everything else, but a suicide note without a suicide is a prologue without a book, an extreme example of pointless literature. Mere mental weightlifting, as Professor Fortuna describes all modern literature. The book would only be ready once she had committed suicide. Unless I saved her first.

And that was when I made my decision. I announced to the Bar do Espanhol that I was going to Frondosa. I just had to persuade Julinha to look after Black the dog. Fulvio Edmar declared that he would come with me – poor Fulvio, if he had consulted the stars about his future, he would still be alive today. He said that he would collect a hundred copies of the new edition of *Astrology and Love* from the printers, sign them and take them with him to Frondosa, where his fans awaited him. Marcito agreed that I should go and, wincing, gave me an advance on my salary. Tavinho, who regretted that he could not come too, helped us prepare our legend, giving us a lecture on five-a-side football and its importance in the provincial towns of Rio Grande do Sul. We would arrive in Frondosa disguised as scouts come from the capital to attend the final of the regional championship and to check out any talented players. The full force of Operation Theseus would be in Frondosa, ready for whatever might happen. After much hesitation, I, too, was ready for enormity.

11

THERE IS NOTHING LIKE AN OVERNIGHT BUS RIDE TO CONCENTRATE the mind. There's nothing like a sleepless night for thinking about the past and imagining the future, as you whizz along the tarmac, as though the road were leading directly – where? To Frondosa to make a book deal, or to Naxos to save a life? Was I an unlikely Dionysus on a rescue mission, or merely an intruder in someone else's labyrinth, a chameleon denying his true nature and wanting to be seen? Ariadne had written that her whole life had been ruled by other people's obsessions – a painter's obsession with a mythical figure, a painter she had never even met; her mother's obsession with her own daughter's youth and beauty; the obsessions of a forbidden lover and of a vengeful husband who had kept her locked away from the world. I would be yet another obsessive interfering in her life. But she had summoned me. She had offered the thread that would lead me to her in order that I might publish her and rescue her, and she had put me on that bus and set me on that road. Only when I arrived would I know if the road led to Frondosa or to Naxos. Quite how my obsession would affect Ariadne, I did not know, nor did I know how it would affect my own destiny. What mattered was that new feeling, the feeling that my life was finally going somewhere, a feeling, they say, very similar to that experienced by a prisoner in a labyrinth just before he bumps into another wall.

"It's all in the stars," said Fulvio Edmar, who was sitting beside me on the bus, trying to convince me of the seriousness of his horoscopes for lovers. The stars determine human behaviour; human behaviour is defined by one's relationships with other people; love and sex are the most extreme forms of relating to someone else – therefore the universe should be read as if it were a relationship counsellor or a vast dating agency, which is precisely what his book was. Knowing that I was a Libra, he needed only to find out Ariadne's sign in order to say how our destinies would entwine and what awaited me at the end of the road. Libra was what he called a "multi-compatible sign", open to all kinds of conjunctions, from "B" to "Z". I had nothing to worry about. There would only be a problem if Ariadne was an Aries or an Aquarius. What kind of problem? He did not answer. He hesitated for a moment, then said, "Be careful."

Whizzing down the road. Me sitting by the window. Fulvio Edmar and his utilitarian universe to my left, the night with its confusion of actual stars to my right. We had embarked with our respective bags, mine containing Ariadne's five original chapters, as well as some clothes and toiletries – including soap, which, according to Dubin, the Frondosa hotel did not supply – and Fulvio's containing a hundred copies of his book, fresh from the printers. Despite its size, Fulvio refused to allow his suitcase full of books to be placed in the luggage locker. He preferred to be able to see it, so it sat alongside mine, occupying several spaces in the luggage rack above our heads. We each wanted to keep an eye on our precious cargo. Then, after having discoursed at length on the scientific seriousness of his work and his plans for further books, such as *Astrology and the Stock Market – A Sidereal Guide for Investors*, Fulvio fell asleep, and I sat gazing out at the starry sky. The same sky that Ariadne used to see through the gaps in the roof of the house of the catalpa tree and which she had described as carbon paper with holes in it, holes that let in "a bonewhite light like death behind all things". The white light that lay behind all things, even the night. The bonewhite eternal light of things that never change. The mysterious light that surrounds us and which we only glimpse through holes made by the stars. I thought about Ariadne's face in that photo of her as a debutante, the only image I would have until I could meet her face to face at the end of the road, ten years on. Her sad smile, a smile that was older than her. The smile the moon would wear if the moon smiled, her Secret Lover had said. Did she already know about the white light behind everything, about death, ever-present, watching us all, even beautiful debutantes with bare shoulders? Was she already a writer then, looking forward to another ten years of life ruled by the obsessions of others and to having a besotted editor to guide her hand and help her write her story? Or was she just a suicide waiting for an excuse?

Whizzing along the tarmac, I was still pondering the fifth chapter of her story in its raw state, unpolished and comma-free. The chapter about that incongruous effigy and the Secret Lover's concrete burial. The Secret Lover had also succumbed to the wretched urge to write, and it had brought about his ruin. That strange compulsion had claimed yet another victim. Professor Fortuna says that instead of worshipping writers, we should praise to the skies the millions who resist and write nothing, and whose great contribution to world literature are the pages they leave blank.

Tavinho had shown me a book of paintings by De Chirico that he had found at home. Ariadne was right: De Chirico was painting loneliness.

The Naxos of his paintings was a vast empty square flanked by desolate arcades that disappeared off into the horizon, and Ariadne, abandoned by Theseus after saving him from the Labyrinth, was a sculpture in the middle of the square. The paintings weren't just images of abandonment, they were a monument to it. Solitude made stone. There was no hope for De Chirico's Ariadne, unless the magic of a Dionysus obsessed with saving her could free her. The sculpture showed Ariadne after she had committed suicide, an Ariadne beyond rescue. What would I do on Naxos with no rescue plan in my bag?

Fulvio had asked if I knew that the constellation Corona Borealis represented the crown that Dionysus had given to Ariadne, and which he had tossed into the sky when she died. I hadn't known that. And I certainly couldn't imitate him. I was, quite clearly, a Dionysus with zero resources.

I must have slept and dreamed, or suffered a brief delirium, because the bus reached its destination twice. The first time, Ariadne was waiting for me in a strange bus station-cum-arcade, wearing the white strapless dress she wore at the debutantes' ball. She greeted me with a smile and open arms. She was two women: the Ariadne of the photograph, only ten years older, and Julinha, thirteen years younger and ready to forgive me. Deeply moved, I embraced them both. The second time, I woke to find that the bus had stopped and Fulvio was struggling to liberate his heavy bag of books from the luggage rack. No-one was waiting for us at the bus station.

In the taxi to the hotel, as a way of establishing our legend, we made a point of speaking only about five-a-side football. The driver agreed that everyone was in a real frenzy about the upcoming match; no-one in the town spoke of anything else. Wanting to show how well informed I was, I said, "I hear Maizena's really play-ing a blinder."

"Maizena? You mean Mandioca."

"Yes, Mandioca. Of course."

The driver eyed me suspiciously, then said, "Everything depends on him." Then: "Are you staying for the game?"

"That's why we're here."

The driver dropped us at the hotel. The square, deserted at that hour of the morning, reminded me of De Chirico's paintings, with their long shadows and sense of desolation. There was the great circle of concrete, like a pedestal waiting for a statue to redeem it. Dubin used to say that the nicest thing about small provincial towns like Santa Edwige dos Aflitos was their ugliness. He was right. Frondosa's ugliness was almost touching. But looking at that empty square, I felt something else too, something magical. I felt removed from the world. The road had carried me further from myself than I had thought. I remembered what Dubin had said about his first impression of Frondosa. It was a place where you would either lose your soul or become a saint. Or a god, I thought. Or a god. I even ran my hand over my face to make sure that my nose and cheeks and eyes were still in their usual places. One thing was sure: I would leave Frondosa a different man from the man I was when I arrived.

After dropping us off, the driver drove round the square to the town hall, where his brother-in-law worked as nightwatchman, and left a message for the mayor, Fabrizio Martelli. The men who were coming to bribe Mandioca had arrived on the night bus from Porto Alegre. He was certain of this. He had immediately felt suspicious of the bags, obviously stuffed with money, from which neither man would be parted, even refusing to put them in the boot of the taxi. But I imagine that his suspicions had been aroused mainly by an attempt made by one of the men to disguise his real intentions by deliberately getting Mandioca's name wrong. When Fulvio and I left the hotel at midday, we were already being followed. But I only found all this out at the end of the story.

12

WALKING THE STREETS OF FRONDOSA WITH LITTLE DUBIN WAS
like touring with a celebrity. Our stroll through the shopping
precinct of Voluntários da Pátria to the Uruguayan's restaurant,
where Dubin enjoyed a free lunch every day, was interrupted
several times by people wanting to shake his hand and, if they
were women, to kiss him. How could Dubin have become so
popular in such a short time?

"I don't know! Charm? Animal magnetism?"

At the restaurant, he was greeted effusively. He embraced a
very plump woman who emerged from behind the bar to welcome
him and introduced her as "Assunta, the love of my life". Assunta
gave a little yelp of pleasure.

"She says she can't marry me because she's already married
and has grandchildren. Free yourself from those bourgeois prejudices, woman!"

Another yelp from Assunta.

The restaurant was decorated entirely in green and yellow, with photos of Brazil's 1950 World Cup team on the walls. We – Dubin, myself, Professor Fortuna and Fulvio – sat at a long table at the back, away from all the other tables, so that we could safely conspire beneath the large photos of Danilo, Ademir and Juvenal. The menu was the same for all of us, starting with cappelletti soup followed by pasta, meat, rice, green salad and potatoes, as well as the restaurant's speciality, roast chicken. Dubin warned us that beer or any other alcoholic drinks would have to be paid for. I ordered some mineral water. Professor Fortuna sat apart from us at the end of the table, despite being told that we would have to speak quietly. This meeting had, after all, been convened in order to plan the next stage of Operation Theseus. The first decision to be made: Should we or should we not reveal our real reason for being there and include people from the town in the Operation? Dubin thought that Paula and her father would make valuable allies. Lúcio Flávio could also help. And it was clear that Ariosto Galotto should be told what had brought us to Frondosa. I agreed only with his last point. I would try to speak to Ariadne's brother myself, if I could manage to catch him when he was sober. The main problem was how to reach Ariadne. Dubin raised one finger: "A question."

"Ask away."

"What exactly do we do when we reach her?"

"We talk to her about the book. We ask if she's ready to publish it and offer her our help."

"A book in which she accuses her husband of having killed her lover?"

"We can publish it as a novel, as a work of fiction. She doesn't mention any names. The only name that appears is hers. And that can be changed."

"But she was the one who gave it the title *Ariadne*, and it's written in the first person. She wants to be identified."

"Well, she does and she doesn't. She wants to reveal the truth and to have her revenge, but, at the same time, she doesn't want them to know that she's writing the book."

The Professor was leafing through the scripts I had brought with me in my bag. Neither he nor Dubin had read the latest chapters Ariadne had sent. The Professor had said nothing up until then, and when he did speak, he surprised us all. He, who had always believed that Ariadne's story was entirely fictitious, had changed his mind.

"Even if you did alter the names, the whole town will know that the story is true. Ariadne has only one way out."

"What's that?"

"To keep her promise and kill herself. That way, she escapes the consequences and the publisher is left with a fine book to be published posthumously. That way, everyone's happy." The Professor was being serious. The Professor never laughs.

"There is another way . . ." I began.

They all looked at me.

"We take her away from Frondosa." I said.

They sat in paralysed silence, Fulvio Edmar with a chicken leg poised halfway between plate and mouth.

After a few seconds, Dubin spoke. "Take her away? You mean kidnap her?"

"It's better than suicide."

Whatever we ultimately did with Ariadne, the problem remained of how to contact her. I suggested recruiting Ariosto Galotto's help. He had lunch with his sister every Thursday. Perhaps he could take one of us with him next time. Surely a guest of his wouldn't be barred from the Martelli household. Or would he? We didn't know if he and Ariadne ate alone or were accompanied by the sombre mother-in-law or by Franco himself. If necessary, Ariosto could take a note from me to Ariadne, arranging a meeting. If he was able to smuggle out his sister's manuscripts and smuggle in my replies, surely he could manage to slip her a furtive note without being caught. But it was dangerous. The Martellis had already killed one brother, and there was nothing to prevent them from killing another. Dubin didn't like the plan. Ariosto Galotto couldn't be relied on. He did his best to remain sober for those Thursday lunches, but his sobriety was so short-lived that it didn't even last until evening. However, Dubin thought that we could perhaps turn Fulvio Edmar's presence to our advantage. We could use him to contact Ariadne, one of his many readers in Frondosa.

Wasn't Fulvio planning to hold a book-signing? Well, why not do it at Fotos Mazaretto? The *Frondosa Folio* could advertise the event, and the Uruguayan would pay for the drinks and canapés. Ariadne would be sure to attend, guarded by her dusky mother-in-law. The place would be mobbed, and he, Dubin, would undertake to distract the mother-in-law with his infallible charm while I talked to Ariadne. We put the idea to the vote, and Dubin's plan won. Two in favour, with me against. The Professor abstained, being too busy eating his green salad.

Assunta came over to our table to make sure Dubin was being well treated. He put his arm about her waist and said, "The only thing I need now is for you to sit on my lap."

Assunta gave another explosive yelp.

When we returned to the hotel, the receptionist asked if, by any chance, one of us was called Agomar. I was about to raise my hand when I remembered that I had signed the register in my real name. Why did she want to know?

"Someone phoned asking to speak to Agomar."

Dubin had given Ariadne a card from the hotel with the name Agomar written on the back.

"Was it a man or a woman?" I asked.

"A man."

In the bar next door to the hotel, Ariosto Galotto, although drunk, was still intelligible. Dubin introduced us. I came straight to the point: "I'm the person you send the white envelopes to, the ones containing your sister's manuscripts."

He stood looking at me, a half-smile playing on his lips, and leaning on a snooker cue that he held grasped in both hands. Finally, he said, "Ah."

"Have you read what she's been writing?"

He waved a hand as if to dismiss the question. "No, no. Well, sometimes I do. I keep the originals and send the copies to you. Sometimes I read what she's written."

"And is what she writes true?"

His half-smile became a full smile, and he asked, "Do you play snooker?"

"Is it true?" I asked again.

Placing the fingers of one hand on my chest, he gave me a gentle shove. "Excuse me. It's my turn to play."

"Do you know what happened to your brother?"

"Augusto? Of course. He left us."

"Yes, but do you know how . . ."

Too late. He was already leaning against the snooker table to play his next shot. Afterwards, completely ignoring me, he went over to the bar to finish off what remained of his brandy.

The chairs placed on the pavement for the hotel's guests were all occupied. After lunch at the restaurant, Fulvio had stayed on at Fotos Mazaretto, where Dubin had introduced him to the owner, old Mazaretto, so that they could make arrangements for the book-signing. The Professor had disappeared. Dubin spotted someone crossing the square and called out: "Rico!" He was right; shaking Rico's hand was just like shaking the hand of a corpse. The dent in his forehead was far deeper than I had imagined. He was younger than I expected too. Medium height, slender physique. He said he was on his way to the town's other hotel, the more modern one, where Mandioca was to remain in preventive quarantine until the match. Rico had made friends with Mandioca at Loló's house and was going to keep him company for a while, because the player was finding confinement hard to bear. Rico had a pack of cards with him.

Dubin took me to see the "Ariadne" building, which had been constructed on the site of the old Galotto house. On the way, he asked, "Are you serious about kidnapping Ariadne?"

"If we're here to save her, then yes."

"Kidnap her and take her where?"

"I don't know."

To my apartment, I thought, where we will finish writing her book, which will be a wild success and will make up for my life as a frustrated man of letters, and where we will live happily ever after, like gods. I will be her editor and her exemplary lover. Editor and writer being another form of incest. All she'll have to do is get used to the impoverished lifestyle of a Dionysus without money or magic. We will live on literature, love and takeaways. If

I ever do toss something up into the sky to become a constellation, it will be in the form of a pizza. I imagined Ariadne laughing at my joke, just as Julinha used to laugh at my jokes when we first started going out together.

"Why do you think Ariosto Galotto didn't want to talk about Ariadne's book and his brother's disappearance?" I asked.

"Because he's afraid. He must be dependent on the Martellis' money."

"But he's helping his sister to get her book published."

"Perhaps he wasn't expecting to see you here and didn't know what to say."

"He said that his brother 'left us'. Is that what you would say about a murdered brother?"

"I can't answer that question. I'm an only child."

The size of the new building gave an idea of how large the demolished house must have been. What had it looked like? Ariadne had described the flagstoned steps at the front, the large salon, the ruined garden, where she had spent her childhood and adolescence and lived out her great forbidden love. The building was a huge gravestone placed on top of the people the Martelli brothers thought were dead and buried. They hadn't counted on Ariadne's nine lives. Nor on that universal compulsion to write.

"You said no-one can remember a catalpa tree growing in front of the house."

"That's what I was told, that there never was a catalpa tree here."

*

Later that afternoon, as I sat outside the hotel, I saw Rico, his face masked, walking across the square in the direction of the cemetery. He was going to Loló's house. His appearance in the square no longer aroused the slightest interest. However, anyone from the town who had bothered to look might perhaps have wondered at the change to his usual trajectory, for, instead of passing in front of his ex-girlfriend's house so that she would know where he was going, he headed straight for the cemetery. But no-one noticed. And I, apparently, was the only one who doubted that the slender figure was the man I had met earlier. It was not Rico. This man walked differently. He walked like a football player.

13

IN HIS COLUMN IN THE *FRONDOSA FOLIO*, LÚCIO FLÁVIO REMARKED on the "cultural ferment" brought to the town by visitors from the capital. The well-known astrologer Fulvio Edmar, author of the best-selling *Astrology and Love*, would be signing copies of his book in Fotos Mazaretto, where, the following day, the celebrated Professor Fortuna would give a lecture on Neoplatonism in the work of Dostoevsky and Machado de Assis. Intelligent life had returned to Frondosa, whose "intellectual scene" – ever since the sale of the Ideal cinema to an evangelical sect – Lúcio Flávio described as "a Sahara with no oases" – or, more precisely, "a square without trees", since nothing symbolised the town's mental aridity better than that great empty concrete "pedestal" in the middle of the square, a monument to nothing. At least for a few days, the local population would have something to think about apart from five-a-side football.

*

That Sunday, Dubin would attempt to speak to Ariadne after the ten o'clock Mass and tell her that Agomar was in town and ready to meet her. Dubin knew he was running two serious risks: being caught talking to Ariadne by her sinister mother-in-law, and becoming a convert to Christianity; he was, however, prepared to make the sacrifice. We were also relying on Ariadne coming to Fulvio's book-signing session. After all, he had been the reason she had chosen us to publish her book, and it had been shown that Fulvio Edmar had a large public in Frondosa. On the day that Lúcio Flávio announced the signing, the newspaper received dozens of phone calls from people wanting to know at what time the event would begin. Professor Fortuna's lecture at the Poets' Club, on the other hand, aroused little interest. According to the Professor, most people's intellectual curiosity barely comes up to their ankles. He was thinking of including in his talk something of what he had learned in India during his immersion course in tantric sex, arguing that both Dostoevsky and Machado de Assis had tantric tendencies. We tried to persuade him that this would not be a good idea.

Paula told us that the church was usually full on Saturday afternoons, which was when Father Bruno heard confession. Most people didn't go in order to confess, but to hear the confessions of others. Father Bruno was so deaf that the faithful had to shout out their sins, and it was not unusual for a murmur to ripple through the assembled crowd whenever a particularly unusual sin issued forth from the confessional, prompted by a *"What?"* from Father Bruno.

"I had impure thoughts about Arlindo, Father."

"You had what?"

"I had impure thoughts about Arlindo!"

"Who?"

Lúcio Flávio hired an informant to remain on duty during confession. She stood close to the confessional and took notes, making a list of all the sins committed by the town's faithful. Lúcio Flávio assured us that Ariadne's confessions were like those of a child. No major sins, not even sins of thought.

Paula was growing suspicious of our intense interest in Ariadne. She could understand Dubin's interest because it was part of his sociological research, but why did I want to know so much about her? Why were we putting out all that bait in order to lure her from the mansion where the monster held her captive? What exactly was it that I needed to say to Ariadne? Who was I? Paula – whom Dubin called "Pa-o-la", so as not to waste the Italian accent he had honed for his role as Nick Stradivarius – thought it all very strange. She didn't even know the true extent of my obsession. She didn't know that I dreamed of Ariadne wearing a white dress.

We went with Paula for lunch at the Uruguayan's restaurant. The restaurant was closed. A note pinned to the door gave the reason:

the Uruguayan had died that morning! The wake for Diamantino Reis was being held at his house, which – to everyone's surprise – was a small wooden affair far from the town centre. The Uruguayan had spent all his money helping others in order to redeem himself for the guilt of having bet against Brazil in the 1950 World Cup, and he lived very modestly. Dubin felt obliged to attend his bene-factor's wake. We went with him in Paula's car. Her father, Afonso, was already there when we arrived, standing beside the coffin. Soon afterwards, Loló, the brothel-keeper, arrived, a short, almost dwarfish woman. I thought at first that she had marked her face with black pencil until I realised that the lines came from the mascara running down her cheeks along with her tears. The Uruguayan's widow received our condolences impassively. No-one knew very much about the Uruguayan's private life. He did not appear to have any children, and, to judge by the house in which he lived and by the modest coffin, the fabulous legacy which, it was assumed, he would leave to the town for charitable works, did not exist. Loló stood on tiptoe to kiss the dead man's face, but couldn't reach. Dubin and I had to lift her bodily off the ground. She did not thank us. Afonso touched my arm, indicated the dead man with a lift of his chin and said, "Engels."

"What?"

"Engels."

Only long afterwards did I understand. He meant Friedrich Engels, the rich industrialist who had supported Marx while the latter was writing his explosive tracts. The Uruguayan was Engels.

His money had supported the *Frondosa Folio*, in which Afonso published his incomprehensible Marxist editorials. Afonso had perhaps not yet realised that, without his Engels, the newspaper was finished.

Even in death, the Uruguayan did not escape Frondosa's old resentment. Few people went to the wake or to the funeral. And mysteriously, once the coffin had been closed, a Uruguayan flag appeared on the lid.

At the end of the afternoon, Dubin and I were sitting side by side in the chairs on the pavement outside the hotel. After a long silence, Dubin, his head back and his eyes closed, said, "This is all a game, isn't it?"

"What do you mean, a game?"

"This town. Us being here. None of it's true, is it? None of it's real."

"It's *surreal*. It's post-De Chirico."

"No, I mean . . . the whole thing. Me and Paula. The false Uruguayan in the coffin. Us lifting Loló up off the floor by her perfumed armpits. And you, for example, what do you intend to do with Ariadne?"

"I intend to publish her book."

"No, you want more than that. And Ariadne isn't real, at least not the Ariadne inside your head, not the one you want to save."

Dubin had not yet read the chapters Ariadne had sent after

he had left for Frondosa. He had merely heard my summary. He lacked a clear idea of the enormity of the situation we had got ourselves into, drawn in, as we were, by the spell cast by Ariadne.

Frondosa was no Santa Edwige dos Aflitos, and Ariadne was no provincial girl charming us with her ingenuous fiction, even if she did write her name with a little flower above the "i". In Frondosa, people died.

I now think of that conversation with Dubin as having been our last opportunity to escape from the ending the stars had prepared for us. Perhaps even Dubin didn't know that he was offering me a way out of my obsession, another ending to the story, an ending in which no-one died and we all kept our innocence. I was about to say that I felt as if the whole of my real life had been merely a prologue to surreal Frondosa when one of Ariosto Galotto's snooker pals arrived with the news, which he announced right there on the pavement, before going into the bar: "Mandioca has escaped from his hotel!"

Mandioca had not come down to breakfast that morning. After Rico, already wearing his mask, had left him the previous evening to go to Loló's house, no-one had seen or heard from Mandioca. The hotel manager had gone into his room, seen a shape under the covers and assumed that the player had decided to sleep in. However, when Mandioca was still under the covers at the end of the afternoon, the manager became concerned. Upon prodding the person in the bed, he discovered it was not Mandioca but Rico.

Mandioca had borrowed Rico's mask and gone straight to Loló's house. And that was where the Martelli brothers and their troop of security guards were heading now. It was then that we learned that the brothers' biggest concern was to find out if Mandioca had had any contact at Loló's house with the men who had arrived on the night bus from Porto Alegre with bags full of money to bribe him with.

Dubin managed to sit behind Ariadne at ten o'clock Mass. He waited for the swarthy mother-in-law to fall asleep so that he could speak to Ariadne, but this time, the mother-in-law remained awake, even during Father Bruno's sermon. Dubin decided to follow Ariadne when she went up to receive Communion, and, standing behind her in the queue, he whispered in her ear that Agomar was in town and eager to talk. Then he himself received the host from Father Bruno, and he could have sworn that, as he walked back to his seat, he heard a chorus of voices, his mother's voice and those of a thousand ancestors, shouting, "What's that boy got in his mouth?!" I remained outside, waiting for my first sight of Ariadne in the flesh. And I did see her. But her face was somehow blurred, just as it had been in my dream. I considered moving closer to get a better look. Our eyes might meet; she might recognise me. Dionysus come to find her, to free her and carry her far from Naxos. Her saviour. Her editor. But she and the swarthy mother-in-law were already moving away from the church in the direction of a car that stood waiting with its doors open. Paula had left the church, roaring with laughter. She couldn't believe it when Dubin got up and joined the queue for Communion. The little fellow was completely mad, which was precisely why she loved him.

Mandioca was back in his hotel room, with extra security this time. Rico, surrounded by a crowd in the pedestrian precinct of Voluntários da Pátria, was explaining his actions. He had done it to help the team, because Mandioca needed sex, a lot of sex, if he was to play well. It was all very scientific, to do with maintaining the correct balance of fluids in his body. The plan was for Mandioca to remain at Loló's house until the day of the match and for Rico to stay at the hotel. How exactly had Rico planned to remain undiscovered during the three days preceding the game? Oh, he said, he would have thought of something. The important thing was for Mandioca to be on top form when he walked onto the pitch. The important thing was for the Galotto team to slaughter their opponents.

Old Mazaretto had, for many years, been the town photographer. According to Paula, no-one in Frondosa officially existed until they had been photographed by Mazaretto making their first Communion, attending a birthday party, coming out as a debutante, graduating or getting married. He had taken the photo of Ariadne as debutante that I carried around with me, close to my heart. But Mazaretto no longer took photographs. He had converted his studio into a shop selling stationery and books, although the latter, mainly of the religious or self-help variety, occupied only two shelves in one corner. The books brought by Fulvio Edmar were piled up near the cash register. Fulvio would be signing them in the backroom, the one Mazaretto hired out to the Poets' Club for their meetings. When we reached the shop, there was already a queue, mostly women, waiting for the author. The plan to serve canapés and drinks during the signing had been abandoned after the Uruguayan's death. Old Mazaretto wouldn't even agree to serve water. I stood guard at the door, waiting for Ariadne to arrive, while Dubin was being introduced to Paula's friends inside, where he soon became the centre of a shrill circle of admirers. At one point, I heard him say, "Yes, I'm Jewish like Jesus Christ, but that's where the resemblance ends." The normally glum Fulvio seemed happy signing books, answering readers' questions and being photographed, but I noticed that few people were buying the new edition of *Astrology and Love*. They almost all wanted Fulvio to sign the old copies they had brought from home. The queue was growing longer, stretching out into the street. Then, suddenly, she appeared. Ariadne. She paused for a moment, framed in the doorway, uncertain whether to go back out again and join the queue or to enter the shop; in the end, she decided to come in and appeared to be heading, oh my God, in my direction. No. She had spotted Paula and Dubin and was going straight over to them. She seemed to be alone, without the dusky mother-in-law and without the escort of wardrobes. Could she have been given a night of freedom? No. Her husband entered immediately afterwards. It could only be him. Franco, with the fine head of hair. The monster. He soon caught her up and grasped her porcelain elbow. I joined Paula and Dubin so as to be part of their group when Ariadne and Franco reached them. I noticed that Franco had left his jacket open so that everyone could see the pistol in the holster at his waist. Ariadne and Paula exchanged kisses, Franco and Dubin shook hands, and Dubin introduced me to Ariadne and Franco. She clasped my hand, her eyes lowered. He tried to crush my fingers in his grasp and nearly succeeded. And before any of us could say anything, he asked, "Is there anyone here called Agomar?"

14

FRANCO MADE SURE THAT EVERYONE SAW HIS GUN. THERE WAS someone called Agomar in town who wanted something from his wife, quite what he didn't know. The card from the hotel that Dubin had given to Ariadne with the name "Agomar" written on the back had been confiscated as soon as she got home. Yes, that's what must have happened. The mother-in-law was just pretending to be asleep, and was, in reality, alert to everything. She had seen Dubin give Ariadne the card. Franco had probably beaten Ariadne to get her to tell him who that Agomar person was. I could see her crying and protesting that she didn't know. "And that Dubin fellow, what does he want with you?" And my poor Ariadne weeping and saying over and over, "I don't know, I don't know!" Now the monster had come to Mazaretto's with his hand in one pocket, so that one side of his jacket was pushed back to reveal the weapon. So that Agomar would know what awaited him.

Dubin and I looked at each other. Dubin asked, "Isn't Fulvio Edmar's real name Agomar?"

"Yes, I think it is," I replied. "Fulvio Edmar is a pseudonym."

"Who's Fulvio Edmar?" the monster asked.

It was Ariadne who answered. "He's the man signing books today, Franco. This book."

She showed him her copy of *Astrology and Love*. "That's why we're here, darling," she went on, looking round and smiling, as if asking us to forgive her husband's stupidity.

We all laughed. I did so with some difficulty, because that "darling" had wounded me. Because Ariadne was even prettier than I had dreamed. Because her smile, however false, had pierced my heart. I felt like shouting, "I'm Agomar!", taking her by the hand and running out into the pedestrian precinct with Franco in hot pursuit, taking potshots at us. Instead, I merely pointed at Fulvio Edmar, who was signing books in a kind of frenzy of euphoria, and said, "There's our author."

When Mazaretto drew Franco to one side to ask him about Mandioca's escape, I took advantage of that pause to move closer to Ariadne. Entering her perfumed aura, I whispered in her perfect ear, "I am Agomar."

She didn't understand. Dubin had introduced me under another name. I didn't attempt to explain. We hadn't much time. Soon, Franco, her owner, would be at her side again. Protecting his porcelain.

"We need to meet to talk about the book."

"Yes." When she spoke, she kept her eyes fixed on Franco, who was now surrounded by a group of people, all wanting to know about Mandioca.

"Where can we meet?" I asked.

"I'll be going to visit my mother's grave tomorrow."

For one wild moment, I thought she was using the town code. Was she going to Loló's house? Was she a regular visitor there? No, of course not. She really was intending to visit her mother's grave.

"At what time?"

"Eleven o'clock."

At eleven o'clock the next morning I would talk to Ariadne about her book. Or at eleven o'clock the next morning I would tell Ariadne that I loved her and had come to save her. At eleven o'clock the next morning ... But we needed to get a few things clear first. Would she be alone at the cemetery?

"Will you be ..." I began.

But she was looking at Franco, who had called across to ask why she wasn't getting her book signed.

"I'm going to, but I can't jump the queue."

"Why not?" the monster roared.

In Frondosa, no Martelli needed to queue for anything, but my Ariadne dutifully went to the back of the queue.

Dubin interrupted Fulvio's frenzied signing to introduce him to Franco. The two men talked. Fulvio couldn't understand why Franco kept calling him by a different name, nor why he used such a threatening tone, smiling all the while, when he said, "So you're this Agomar fellow, are you?" Nor the way in which he said, having first attempted to crush Fulvio's fingers when he shook his hand, that he didn't believe in all that astrology guff. Then Franco talked to Dubin. He wanted to know how his research was going, if Dubin had reached any conclusions, and if he and his brother Fabrizio would emerge as the villains of the piece in Dubin's account of how the Galotto factory had changed hands. Later on, Dubin told me that Franco had also asked who I was, and that he'd invented a legend for me on the spot. I was a geologist investigating the theory that a meteor had struck the earth, leaving behind it a deep crater, at the exact point where, millions of years later, Frondosa would spring up. The soil in Frondosa must therefore contain traces of material from the meteor, material unknown anywhere else in the world. Particles from the explosion would also still be hanging about in the air around the town, which would explain its unique character. Franco, Dubin said, was surprised, because he had been under the impression that Agomar and I had come to Frondosa to see the five-a-side final.

I was standing by the table where Fulvio was signing books when Ariadne's turn came. He stood up to greet her. She praised his work. It was hard to believe that Ariadne, who spoke several languages, who could tell a Monet from a Manet, who liked poetry and whose luminous prose had enchanted me from the very first sentence, despite the spelling mistakes and the lack of commas, should be an admirer of Fulvio Edmar. But there she was, saying, "I'm a great admirer of yours," and asking him if he also did birth charts, and him asking her if she would like him to do hers. And the two of them arranging – far from Franco's ears – for him to visit her house to do just that. And her giving Fulvio her address and saying, "Saturday afternoon then. I'll leave orders for them to let you in," and me, captivated, studying her profile and thinking, when she's mine, we'll improve her literary tastes. Besides, what did Ariadne expect to see in the stars? Her own suicide?

Fulvio asked, "What sign are you?"

"Aquarius," my beloved replied.

At eleven o'clock the next morning, I was in Frondosa cemetery. It wasn't hard to spot Ariadne – I could see her from some way off. She was standing alone by a mausoleum. I assumed that no guard was considered necessary on her visits to the cemetery. No sinister mother-in-law was in sight, no wardrobes. The tomb where she had just placed some flowers belonged to the Galotto family. The previous night, she had spoken only of "my mother's grave", not "my parents'" or "my family's" grave. Perhaps the visits and the flowers were for her mother alone, in order to ease her guilt. I remembered what she had written about her mother not forgiving her before she died. And about how she missed having a close, understanding mother instead of one as distant as a dark moon, to bless her children and forgive their forbidden love. She had come to the cemetery to exorcise her guilt and seek forgiveness.

Perhaps that explained the absence of any guards. The tyrannical Franco respected his wife's painfully personal moments. Or perhaps the guards were hiding. Distrust every shadow, le Carré had taught me.

Ariadne received me with a smile and a handshake, but she didn't look me in the eye.

I adopted a jovial tone. "So, when are we going to publish your book?"

She shook her head. "The book isn't ready."

"Will it only be ready when you . . ." I hesitated. How to put that thought into words: When you kill yourself? I tried to think of another way of putting it, but that proved unnecessary. She was no longer listening. I noticed that visitors had suddenly appeared out of nowhere beside the graves on either side of the Galotto vault.

"They're Franco's security guards. You'd better leave," she muttered.

"But what about our book?"

"We'll talk later."

"Listen . . ." I moved closer to her, and whispered, "We're going to get you out of here."

"What?"

"Prepare yourself. We're going to take you away."

"What do you mean, 'take me away'? Who is?"

"Make yourself ready."

She moved farther off and pretended to be rearranging the flowers on the tomb. I left the cemetery through the gate near Loló's house. If Franco asked me about that meeting, I would say it was pure chance, that I had been walking through the cemetery on my way to Loló's and had simply stopped to say hello to Dona Ariadne.

The guards came after me. Only later on did I discover that they weren't watching Ariadne, they were following me. They were keeping an eye on me in case I attempted to bribe Mandioca.

It was impossible to miss Loló's house on the street that backed on to the cemetery. The pumpkin-orange house stood out from the other hovels like a gold tooth in a mouthful of rotten stumps. Wearing a worn silk robe and with traces of mascara still on her cheeks from the tears she had shed for the Uruguayan, Loló herself opened the door and said irritably, "You're a bit early, aren't you?" Then she told me to come in and wait; she would wake up one of her girls. I spent the rest of the morning talking to the young woman whom Professor Fortuna had met on the bus and who told me about the tantric sex he practised. There was no physical contact. The man and the woman sat opposite each other and exchanged emanations, erotic waves, which, at least in theory, provoked multiple orgasms. With one finger she stroked the scar above my left eye – Corina's work – and invited me to go up to her room for some proper sex. I thanked her, but refused. The money that Marcito had given me for Operation Theseus would not stretch to such extravagances, even allowing for the discount offered to morning visitors. When I left Loló's house, I saw that Franco's security guards had improvised a football game to while away the time, kicking a beer can around in the middle of the street. We crossed the empty cemetery, on our way back to the centre of town, in single file.

Our doubts as to whether to recruit Paula, her father, Lúcio Flávio and the many other Frondosa inhabitants hostile to the Martelli brothers were resolved by Professor Fortuna. If the outcome of this story was preordained by the stars, then Professor Fortuna was clearly acting as their agent in the spectacular way in which he precipitated events. His talk at the Poets' Club was on Friday night. By the end of Saturday evening everything that was going to happen had happened. Blame the stars. Blame that madman. Blame me. Above all, blame literature.

On that Friday, very few people turned up to hear Professor Fortuna in the small backroom where the Poets' Club held their meetings. Not even the club's president was there. Rico had had to go into hiding after being accused of upsetting the town's star player before the decisive match; he had also been threatened with a bullet in the other temple – just to see if that, too, would ricochet – if the Galotto team lost on Saturday. The Professor's talk was en-titled "Neoplatonism in Dostoevsky and Machado de Assis", but the only reference he made to those writers was the surprising observation that their styles had much in common because they were both mulattos.

After vigorously rubbing the sides of his nose, Professor Fortuna had begun with a categorical statement: "Literature ended with Sophocles. Everything that came after is a mere postscript." He then went on to provoke a groan of revolt from Lúcio Flávio by proclaiming that the only good thing about Proust was that he had given asthma a literary reputation.

Truly revolting, though, for the female majority in the audience, was the Professor's statement that it was unwise to teach women to read and write, because this brought with it the risk that they might become writers, whom he described as highly dangerous individuals. This was when Dubin and I were finally persuaded that the Professor was mad. The Professor himself became aware of the indignation he had caused and tried to make amends by saying that some female writers redeemed the species in general and made up, with their talent, for the devastation they wrought. Besides, they might not know it, but an excellent young woman writer was growing up in their midst, Ariadne Martelli, whose first book, he believed, deserved comparison with the work of the Hungarian authoress Ivona Gabor.

Paula did not wait for the Professor to finish his lecture before demanding an explanation. Ariadne was writing a book?! What was that all about?! We promised to tell her everything, but not there. We left and went in search of a table in a bar somewhere.

Friday night in the pedestrian precinct bars wasn't the best of times to find the ideal conditions for such major revelations. We finally found a reasonably discreet corner, where we all crammed around a tiny table, Paula, her father, Lúcio Flávio, Dubin, Fulvio and me. The Professor had stayed behind at the Poets' Club to confront an increasingly irate public. The last thing we had heard him say, in answer to a question from the floor, was that Virginia Woolf should have been shot.

Dubin began. He told them about how the manuscripts had arrived at the office. About our decision to investigate their origin. About his coming to Frondosa as a spy. Yes, he had lied to Pa-o-la. He apologised, but explained that everything he had done had been for the sake of the mission. Even taking Communion. Then it was my turn to talk about Ariadne's book. It wasn't a book. It was a testament, a confession, a denunciation. Ariadne had had an affair with her youngest brother, Augusto. Her husband had found out and ordered that her brother be killed. He had then kept Ariadne prisoner, under constant guard, so that she would not reveal what she knew and would not escape his control. However, he had reckoned without literature. Ariadne had started writing her terrifying secret story and then sent it to a publisher with the help of her older brother. She described her encounters with Augusto in the house of the catalpa tree, their nights of love beneath a sky that reminded her of a perforated sheet of carbon paper, the death of her "secret lover", everything. She said that at the end of her story, when her vengeance was complete, she would commit suicide. But I was there to save her. Then I corrected myself: *we* were there to save her. And now that they knew everything, we were counting on Paula, Afonso and Lúcio Flávio to help us in our mission, which, after Professor Fortuna's indiscretion, had taken on a new urgency. The next day, everyone in town would know that Ariadne was writing a book. Franco would know. He might even find out that very night. Ariadne's life was in immediate danger. We needed to act.

Nothing horrified our new accomplices more than the news that the angelic Augusto might be buried beneath the concrete circle in the square. They all remembered how the ghastly thing had been put in place in great haste, overnight, and how Ariadne's younger brother had simply disappeared. Once she had recovered from the shock, Paula realised that if the Martelli brothers were accused of murder, there would then be a legal reason for removing the concrete circle. They would destroy it with pickaxes! Afonso cheered up at the thought of being able to write scorching editorials about the scandal, which was neither more nor less than a reflection of the moral crisis affecting an entire class. And Lúcio Flávio saw, at last, a chance of glory in the articles he would write about the affair, which was sure to attract nationwide attention. He summed up the feelings of all three in just one word: "Fantastic!" They all agreed that we had to act. But how?

*

Ariadne had arranged for Fulvio Edmar to visit her in order to draw up her birth chart on the afternoon of the following day, on Saturday, the day of the five-a-side final. That meant she would not be going to the match with her husband. Perhaps she would excuse herself by saying that she had a migraine. Fulvio Edmar would be our key man, I said. Our man inside, deep inside. He would be charged with freeing Ariadne from the monster's lair.

"Me?!" Fulvio said. "No fear!"

We ignored him. He would convince Ariadne to leave the house with him. He could say that it was written in the stars, that the stars were ordering her to flee.

"Mention the Eastern star," I told him. "Tell her she must follow the Eastern star."

We would be waiting close by, in Paula's car. We would take Ariadne to some safe place, perhaps to Afonso's house in the country, until we could get her out of the area. It wasn't a perfect plan, but there was no time to come up with a better one.

Paula asked if she could read Ariadne's manuscript. I said I would give it to her the next morning, on one condition: that she would not let Dubin near enough to the text to start adding commas.

15

"SYLVIA PLATH."

"What?"

"Sylvia Plath. Ariadne copied entire lines from Sylvia Plath."

Paula was holding the plastic file containing Ariadne's manuscript in one hand and a book in the other. It was the next day, and we were sitting in the hotel foyer on old armchairs upholstered in velvet, or what had once been velvet. Dubin was watching me anxiously, not knowing how I would react to what Paula was about to show me.

"Look," she said.

She had underlined in pencil the parts that had been copied: "If the moon smiled she would resemble you . . ."; "Dying is an art like everything else . . ."; "It drags the sea after it like a dark crime . . ." It was all in the book she was holding: the Complete Poems of Sylvia Plath, in English.

"Is there any mention of an effigy?" I asked.

"Yes, that's what made me suspicious. I knew I'd read that line somewhere about an effigy gentled by candles. I went to find the Sylvia Plath book that Ariadne brought back for me from Europe years ago. And there it was. Along with the phrase 'a golden child' that she uses about the 'Secret Lover', and 'I am ready for enormity . . .'"

"She invented the whole story," Dubin said gently, as if he were bringing me news of a death.

"Another thing," Paula went on. "There was never a catalpa tree outside the Galotto house. And Ariadne's mother was nothing like the mother she describes. Poor Dona Ritinha. Pure invention."

I felt as if I had been eviscerated. I thought: So this is what people mean by "an inner void". I tried to speak, but I had no lungs, no diaphragm. I remember nodding several times, a silent "yes" that meant, Fine, let's go home, it's all over. My fault for failing to understand the significance of that little flower above the "i". But it wasn't over yet.

It was gone four o'clock in the afternoon. Paula had spent all morning, first reading and re-reading Ariadne's text, then looking for the Sylvia Plath book, then comparing the text with the poems. By the time she and Dubin arrived at the hotel, I had dispatched Fulvio Edmar to Ariadne's house. Franco wouldn't be there at that hour, because the five-a-side final started at four. And it was likely that the Martelli brothers' security guards would also be at the sports centre so as not to miss the match. In order to get Ariadne out of the house, Fulvio would only have the dusky mother-in-law to deal with. We would be waiting nearby in Paula's car to carry Ariadne off and hide her. Except that now we needed to stop Fulvio or find some way of telling him that everything had changed. Ariadne's story was a work of fiction. At that moment, he was the most vulnerable character in the whole espionage plot, the agent who has lost contact with base and does not know that the plan has been aborted.

Paula drove, Dubin rode in the front seat, and I, reduced to a mere carcass, sat in the back. The street was strangely busy. People shouting. A crowd emerging from the sports centre, as if the match had ended. But that was impossible; the game had only begun a short while ago, it couldn't have ended already. Someone was screaming, "Kill him! Kill him!" People were filling the street, blocking us in.

Paula stuck her head out of the window to ask, "What's going on?"

Someone answered furiously, "Mandioca gave the game away!"

"What do you mean?"

"He deliberately screwed up. He scored two own goals in the first ten minutes."

"And the game's over?"

"Play was suspended before the end of the first half. The

fans invaded the pitch to get Mandioca. It was a real mess. He's probably still running."

To travel from the hotel to Ariadne's house would normally take fifteen minutes. It took us nearly an hour. And with the match suspended, and assuming he wasn't one of those pursuing Mandioca, we knew that Franco would nearly be home, where he would find Ariadne with Fulvio or, as he believed, with Agomar.

We parked outside the house. The big gates were closed. We didn't know if Franco was home yet or not. We saw two cars in the driveway behind the iron fence. One of them could have brought Franco back from the sports centre. What should we do? Ring the bell and wait? But wait for what? For Fulvio to come racing, terrified, out of the gates or else walking calmly towards us . . . Then we heard the sound we were afraid we would hear, the sound none of us had dared to mention, but that we were all expecting. A shot. Then another.

The square was packed with people. Professor Fortuna was watching it all, goggle-eyed, from the entrance to the hotel. We told him what had happened. We had hesitated after hearing the shots. Should we stay or should we go? Staying wouldn't get us anywhere. If what we imagined had actually happened, they were hardly going to let us into the house. We waited to see if anyone left. No-one did. The silence that followed the shots was the ominous silence of the grave. Paula made a decision: she would drop us off at the hotel, then go and find her father. Afonso would know what to do.

I flung myself down in one of the threadbare armchairs and closed my eyes.

Two shots. What had we done? The noise from the square was a constant low hum from which, now and then, an angry word emerged. What were they shouting? In the distance, above the roar from the square, I heard a siren. An ambulance! An ambulance had been called to the Martellis' house. A sign that no-one was dead, only injured. Two shots. Two casualties. Or one person injured by two shots. Where was Dubin? I needed to give him the good news. No-one had died. We were saved.

The sound coming from the crowd had increased in volume. It had grown closer. I could make out what they were saying now. "There he is!" I heard someone yelling. I opened my eyes. A fat, shirtless man had appeared at the hotel window and was pointing in my direction: "That's him!" The words formed sentences, but the sentences made no sense: "He was the one who brought the money here to bribe Mandioca. There he is!" I recognised the taxi driver who had driven us from the bus station. More people appeared at the foyer window and at the hotel entrance. Those behind them were craning their necks to see: "Who is it? Who is it?" And the fat, shirtless man kept repeating, "That's him over there!"

*

I raced up the stairs. I would lock myself in my room and repel the attacking hordes with whatever weapons came to hand. What did they mean by saying that I had brought the money to bribe Mandioca? Who did they think I was? On the stairs I met Dubin coming down, carrying the suitcase he had taken with him when he left Porto Alegre, now full of the trousseau given him by the Uruguayan.

"Let's get out of here!" he shouted. "Grab your things!"

"I don't reckon anyone was killed, you know. I think they were only wounded. I heard an ambulance . . ."

"Fine, fine, but let's get going."

"How? The hotel's under siege. There's no escape."

"There's a rear entrance."

"What then?"

"I don't know. We'll find Paula. She can drive us to the bus station."

"But the foyer's full of people. They're out to get me!"

"Because of Ariadne?"

"No, because of Mandioca!"

Dubin didn't understand.

"Mandioca?"

But there was no time to explain.

"Alright, alright. You can tell me later. Now go and get your bag!"

*

I grabbed my bag and went down the stairs, expecting to find a mob waiting in the foyer, ready to lynch me. Instead, at the foot of the stairs, I saw Túlio's kindly, swarthy face. He had just arrived. Dubin had already told him what had happened, and he agreed that it was best if we left. He would drive us to Porto Alegre. Were we ready? We just had to pay the hotel bill. And find Professor Fortuna.

I think the only reason the hordes didn't invade the hotel was because they were intimidated by Túlio's sheer size. Nonetheless, we paid the bill to shouts of "Bastard!" and "We'll get you, you son of a bitch!" Dubin had trouble settling his account with the hotel manager. The Uruguayan had paid part of his bill in advance, but not all of it. Dubin said that he would borrow some money from Paula and return shortly. We had arranged to leave by the back entrance and for Túlio to pick us up in a side street. What about the Professor? We couldn't wait. My life was in danger. The Professor would have to take care of himself. While Túlio left by the front entrance, cutting a swathe through the crowd with his large frame, Dubin and I headed for the back door. And thus we fled Frondosa. A sad end to Operation Theseus.

Whizzing back down the motorway to Porto Alegre in Túlio's car, I tried not to think about those two shots, and about what might have happened in the Martelli household. Franco arriving back from the match, absolutely furious, and finding Ariadne with Fulvio Edmar, whom he believed to be the man sending secret messages to his wife, and ... And then what? Did he shoot Fulvio? Did he shoot them both? I tried not to think about it. I tried to obliterate Frondosa from my thoughts as if it had ceased to exist, as if it had been struck by a meteor like the one invented by Dubin, or as if the volcano supposedly responsible for the region's topography had erupted again and smothered my guilt in ashes. I looked out at the stars. The holes in the sky letting in the bonewhite light, which, according to Ariadne – or Sylvia Plath – was like the death behind all things.

"Which one is the Corona Borealis?" I asked.

"I don't think you can see it from here," Túlio said. "Only in the northern hemisphere."

Just as well, I thought. At least there wouldn't be a whole constellation above my head to remind me of Ariadne.

* * *

Very little was reported in the press. If it hadn't been for the fact that one of the deceased was the astrologer Fulvio Edmar, it would have been dismissed as a regrettable domestic incident, as the judge presiding over the case described it – a judge who, as it happened, often played cards with the Martelli brothers at the club. Shots fired by mistake at a supposed assailant – well, it happens every day, it hardly merits much attention. And although there will always be malicious people who will make things up and say the story isn't true, that it was a crime of passion and so on, the fact is that only Fulvio Edmar's death made the news. Ariadne's death was much regretted. People shook their heads imagining her husband's grief when he discovered that he had killed his own wife, such a lovely young woman. But that was all. As the judge said succinctly, when he closed the case, "These things happen."

For some time, Dubin kept in touch with Paula, by letter and by phone. She told him everything that happened after our flight from Frondosa, after the sad end of Operation Theseus. She described how Fulvio and I, for some reason, were suspected of having brought in money with which to bribe Mandioca. They still didn't know if Mandioca had, in fact, been bribed to give away the game or if he had simply rebelled against their treatment of him, locking him in his hotel room like an animal, thus interfering with his sex life and preventing him from maintaining the correct balance of bodily fluids that guaranteed his performance on the pitch. No-one knew what had become of Mandioca. Some said he was playing for a team in a town in deepest Paraná, under another name. Others said that the crowd had caught up with him that afternoon and that he would never play again. Rico had disappeared as well. Ah yes, and the game interrupted by the pitch invasion had been cancelled and replayed on another day. Before the replay, a minute's silence had been observed in honour of Dona Ariadne, the wife of the team's director–owner. The Galotto team had won even without Mandioca and were declared regional champions.

*

Paula also described the scene at the Galotto family vault during Ariadne's funeral. Augusto, her younger brother, had made the trip from Santa Catarina, where he ran a beach kiosk. He was still wearing a ring in his nose. Ariosto, her older brother, completely drunk, had insisted on giving a speech in which, if Paula had understood him rightly, he had attacked the passing of time. Paula could only remember one phrase: "One generation going, another coming. It has to stop!" During the funeral, Franco wept bitterly, but after the Galotto team's victory, he was seen punching the air as he was carried in triumph on the shoulders of his security guards, along with his brother Fabrizio.

Paula had promised Dubin that she would come to Porto Alegre so that their love, born among insects and ticks, would not die. But she never came. Over time, their letters and phone calls grew fewer and fewer. In one of her last letters, Paula summarised everything we had left behind in Frondosa, the debris, so to speak, of Operation Theseus. Without the Uruguayan's support, her father had had to close down the newspaper and now devoted himself exclusively to his experiments with roses. He was trying to create an extraordinarily red rose, which he would call Rosa Luxemburg. He had bade farewell to journalism with an outspoken editorial inveighing against the moral decadence of the bourgeoisie and the corruption of the world in general; it ended with a protest against the negligence of the local judge in refusing to investigate the deaths at the Martelli house. Franco, the killer, went free despite the curious fact that, when the supposed assailant was shot, he was engaged in drawing up a birth chart for the lady of the house. Without the Uruguayan's help, Loló had to close her house. She was threatening to write a book revealing everything about her life and her clients. So even Loló – who would have thought it? – had succumbed to the temptations of literature. Lúcio Flávio would be helping her and had already announced that he hoped to lend a Proustian tone to her memoirs. Father Bruno had been replaced by a younger priest who could hear perfectly well, thus saving the local sinners from any embarrassment when they went to confession. And Professor Fortuna was still in Frondosa! He was teaching a course on oriental philosophy, which included classes in tantric group sex that involved no physical contact and used what he called "Orgiastic Distance". The hideous concrete circle remained in place, resisting Ariosto Galotto's nightly sprinkling of urine; worse still, a survey revealed that most of Frondosa's population preferred it to the tree it had replaced and would probably vote to re-elect Fabrizio Martelli.

Dubin's students could not understand the change in their teacher when he returned. There were no more games, no more fun-filled classes performed in a variety of voices, such as his unequalled imitation of Yogi Bear explaining metaphony. Even the beautiful Bela complained that Dubin no longer pestered her with his daft attempts at seduction and had become very dull and serious. We still meet at the Bar do Espanhol, but spend most of the time in silence, trying to get drunk as quickly as possible. So much so that the Spaniard occasionally complains, "What, no more fights?" and threatens to expel us from the bar for good behaviour. The other day, I asked Dubin if he had any news from Santa Edwige dos Aflitos, but he merely smiled and said, "A strange place, the provinces, a strange place," and nothing more. We never talk about Frondosa. It's as if it had been struck by a meteor and all that remained were a few archaeological curiosities, things without soul or life that have nothing to do with us. Tavinho sometimes tries to get us to reveal details of the failed operation, but we always change the subject. My Monday-morning hangovers have returned, and my rejection letters have become even more violent. I decided to get my spy novel out of the drawer and discovered that I had named my main character, the journalist who uncovers the American conspiracy to sabotage Brazil's nuclear programme, Agomar Peniche. I'm thinking of inventing a pseudonym for the author and recommending that Marcito publish the book. In fiction you can meddle in your characters' lives as much as you want. You can even kill them, if you wish. With no guilt, no remorse – and no accidents. Or you can save them.

To my surprise, Marcito paid for Fulvio Edmar's body to be brought back and buried in Porto Alegre. We put a death notice in the newspaper, but no-one came to the funeral – no relative, no friend, none of his thousands of readers. Dubin and I were the only ones there. However, the news of the author's death-by-error revived

LUIS FERNANDO VERISSIMO is a satirist, cartoonist, translator, television writer, saxophonist, playwright and novelist. With over sixty published titles, he is one of the most popular of contemporary Brazilian writers.

MARGARET JULL COSTA is the award-winning translator of José Saramago, Javier Marías, Bernardo Atxaga, Eça de Queiroz and Fernando Pessoa.

NELLY DIMITRANOVA is an artist and illustrator who has lectured in life drawing at Bath Spa University College and exhibited at the Royal Academy.

ACKNOWLEDGEMENTS

Lines from "Lady Lazarus", "The Moon and the Yew Tree", "The Rival", "Mary's Song", "Insomniac" and "A Birthday Present" taken from *Collected Poems* © Estate of Sylvia Plath and reprinted by permission of Faber and Faber Ltd.